This book belongs to

First Published 1990 by
Poolbeg Press Ltd.
Knocksedan House,
Swords, Co Dublin, Ireland.

ISBN 1 85371 074 1

Cover design by Pomphrey Associates.
Printed by the Guernsey Press Ltd.,
Vale, Guernsey, Channel Islands.

The Caravan

The Caravan

Michael Mullen

Children's
POOLBEG

To Eleanor Powers

Contents

1
The Labyrinth

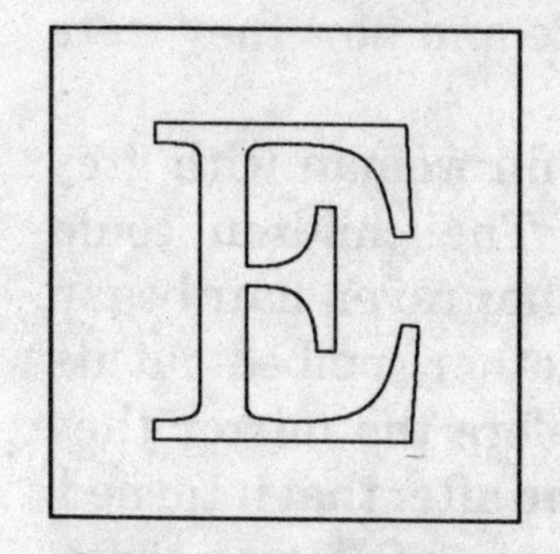

ach evening, as the light was beginning to fail in the huge estate the children pulled the curtains. They pulled them upon their own poverty and fear. For the children there never seemed to be a time when there was not poverty and fear. Poverty was as deep in their minds as the cold in their bones.

Michael Carney and his sister Maeve stood on the high chairs and drew the curtains along the blue rope until they joined in the centre. They looked cautiously on to the street, hoping that the Shark and his gang would not come beating down the door of the house that night. The gang had already broken some of the windows and these had been replaced with thin plywood which did not protect them from either the cold or the wind. The Shark and his gang followed Michael and Maeve into their dreams and often they called out in terror from their sleep.

They finished their task. They felt a little more secure. They had sealed off the house from the life of the great estate and now they were alone with their mother.

Ellen Carney was a thin woman with grey hair and a lined face. The children could remember the day when her raven hair began to turn grey. As their mother combed out its strong tangled length before the mirror they noted the first grey rib. And after that it turned, strand by strand, as ill fortune fell upon them.

They could recall each event on the downward path to poverty. Their father had died in a car crash on the Clontarf road. The offenders did not even incur a jail sentence. Neither the driver nor their father was insured. The Carneys were left without security or money.

That was the beginning of the tragedy. Soon their mother began to sell her small possessions. At first she sold the silver combs which bound her black hair. Then she sold her engagement ring and her wedding ring. Poverty began to be a stark presence in the house.

"If I were by the sea I could live well," she told them. "I would feel certain and secure there and I would want for little. But here in this warren of houses, each and every one the same, my eyes and my mind grow weary and I feel that I am caught in a labyrinth. Little did I think when I was a free and easy girl that I would end up here."

The children did not miss the rings and the silver comb. However when the oak sideboard disappeared and left only an outline on the wallpaper and an empty space, they felt that they were beginning to be poor. After that the house became progressively more bare. Their mother had to borrow in order to pay the rent. Soon they had to have recourse to the Shark.

The children had nightmares about the Shark. He was always there, larger than life. He wore a wide-brimmed artistic hat, a huge coat with a fur-lined collar and his nose was pickled blue from whiskey. On his right hand was a gold ring with a gold sovereign set upon it and he smelt of perfume. He was vast and corpulent and he drove a Mercedes with two steer horns projecting from the chrome bumper, all the better to terrorise the families in the estate.

The Shark lived in loud splendour in the

original Manor House among trees at the edge of the estate. He had torn down the fine entrance with its square pillars and family crest. It was replaced by hideous pine stakes and a crossbeam from which hung the new name of the place, "Tumbleweed House." People had complained about the destruction of the great gates but they all had withdrawn their objections when the Shark hired rough men to threaten them. He always hired men to threaten people.

One of the roughest of his henchmen was Gumpus Cackle. Nobody really knew why he was called this but it had been his name from his earliest days. He used to disappear from time to time. The usual story was that things had got too hot for him and that he had shipped on a coaster to escape the law. He talked like a sailor, you see. But most people believed it was because he often took the blame for any clearly criminal act that the Shark's gang were guilty of and so he knew the inside of most jails in the country. The Shark's clients always breathed a sigh of relief when he vanished. Bad as the Shark was on his own, when Gumpus Cackle was in tow the pair of them were really evil and terrifying. The word was that he was on his way back and the Shark's evil smile seemed to confirm this.

"Don't have recourse to the Shark, Mrs Carney. Whatever you do, don't have recourse to the Shark," a neighbour implored her when she had no one to turn to for money.

"And leave the children starve and go without?" she replied. "I'll get a short term loan and then pay it back and that will be the end of my dealings with the Shark."

"So you say now, but once you get caught in that fellow's net you'll never get out. Mark my words Mrs Carney."

The Shark moved like a great predatory fish through the huge estate, his large form slumped luxuriously behind the wheel, his eyes seeking out the weak and the unfortunate—the people who came to him as a last resort.

Michael and Maeve remembered the day the Shark arrived at the house. He emerged from the huge car and walked up the small garden path to the house. He knocked at the door. When their mother opened it his vast frame blocked out the light.

They listened from the kitchen while the deal was done in the sitting room. The Shark talked a lot about interest on money, which Michael understood from school. He knew even then that the Shark was asking for huge returns on his money. And then before the money was handed over the Shark gave this warning: "I will have your last drop of blood and the very skin off your body if the payments fall too far behind. If this happens you will pay interest on interest, and then you will pay interest on interest on interest. And there is no escape from this house and this estate."

After the Shark had made his exit, the children came back into the sitting room. Their mother was holding a wad of dirty pound notes. Her face was ashen with fear. "I think I made a mistake," she said. She counted out the money to them on the coffee table. Then when they were certain that they had one hundred pound notes their mother set the money out in six piles: one for the rent, the second for the gas, the third for the electricity, the fourth for clothes, the fifth for food and twenty pounds as a standby. The little piles of dirty notes looked insignificant and they did not know then that they would be the cause of much hardship. Michael would never forget the soiled money. It was frayed and limp and stained. It had been clutched and bent and balled in the weak hands of the poor and he felt that some of it had been stained with tears.

The money only served to stay their poverty

for a month. At the end of the month the Shark arrived for his first ten pounds repayment. Mrs Carney had not expected him and she did not understand his talk about interest. But he explained the principle of interest using his large fingers. He had arrived on the day when she drew the children's allowance so she had some money on hand.

"And remember you still owe me one hundred pounds," he told her as he went out the door. Mrs Carney did not understand his methods.

But then the house began to grow bare. The carpets were sold and they were followed by the large table in the front room. Then Mrs Carney sold the record player and finally the television had to go. Soon nothing remained. To entertain Michael and Maeve, Mrs Carney began to read from her small library. Each evening as they huddled together in the back room beside an oil stove she began to read the great myths and legends. And suddenly the world was transformed. She read of the fate of the Children of Tuireann, the wooing of Etáin, the combat at the ford, about Deirdre and the Sons of Usna. The children were no longer confined to the huge estate. Their imaginations took wing and their hearts became warm. They did not feel time pass or the night deepen or the cold enter their bones.

And she also read travel books. On the map they plotted the course of Columbus as he sailed to America and Vasco Da Gama as he sailed around the tip of Africa and they wept for Alexander the Great when he had no more lands to conquer.

Michael and Maeve said afterwards that it was these great stories which helped them over the hard winter, when the heavy snow covered the estate and when the had only bread to eat and milk to drink.

But they could never shake off the spectre of the Shark. By now Mrs Carney owed him three hundred pounds. She could not understand how she got into this amount of debt but it weighed heavily upon her. Sometimes she wept with shame and frustration.

"I come from good people in the West. We never owed money to anyone and we could always hold our heads high. Now look at the state I am in and the debt into which I have fallen. If only I could find some way of getting out of this labyrinth and getting back to the cottage by the sea. It is still there waiting for me with forty acres of land. Your grandfather keeps it well." As they talked they often imagined what life might be like close to the great Atlantic, in a snug cottage, while the storms and the waves roared madly in the bay.

"It is only a dream. Only a dream and there is no way we will ever make the journey now. We must remain here. Spring will come soon and we will not even notice the flowers open, the buds split and young leaves unbind," the mother commented sadly.

January passed slowly and so did February. March came and began to soften into April. The Carneys' plight became worse, but then fortune, which had not looked favourably upon them, now took a strange and unexpected turn.

Every Friday Mrs Carney went to the post office to collect the family allowance. On this Friday it was crowded as usual as it was too small for the large estate it was supposed to service. All the women about her were non-descript and their expressions bore the tight marks of quiet desperation. They lined up in a long silent file shaped like a narrow U and shuffled along when the position at the counter became vacant.

Finally Mrs Carney's turn arrived. She handed in her two allowance books and waited in humiliated silence. As it happened there was a single pound note among the cash she received. "And I'll have a lottery ticket," she said, feeling that she was being extravagant. The assistant took the pound and slid the silver ticket out under the grid to her. She put it in her bag with her money.

As she was returning home she had to pass by an itinerant camp thrown up on the side of the road and close to open fields. She noted the trailers drawn into an awkward line. The place looked dishevelled with clothes lines, piles of batteries and small hills of rusty scrap. And then she came to the caravan. It was barrel-shaped with a pipe for a chimney. The painted motifs on the side and the doors were faded and the tackling and chains had surface rust. But she could see that it was in good condition. And hanging on the half door was a sign with bright red letters, FOR SALE.

Mrs Carney had never been inside a caravan before. She mounted the steps and looked inside. The tunnel of darkness was lit by the door and a window in the back. The space was empty except for two bunks without mattresses and a small table. It had a musty smell and there were some bags filled with scrap on the floor. She gazed in wonder at the inside of the caravan. It recalled memories of her childhood which she had suppressed or forgotten.

Pictures and images began to return. She saw a caravan, with pots and pans suspended from the underfloor, making its way past the house by the sea. The traveller Tom Ward stopped at the gate and talked to her father. Sometimes he spent a day about the house and then left for some destination beyond the hill: some town or fair or gathering.

There was a sound behind her. She turned around. A young man was standing in the doorway. He looked suspiciously at her.

"Well do you intend to buy it? We've got an offer for it," he said brusquely.

"Oh no. I was passing the road and I saw the FOR SALE sign. I have never been in a caravan before so I thought I might peer inside. I once remember Tom Ward's caravan passing by the house at home," she answered.

When she mentioned the name Tom Ward the man's hostility lessened. "This is the very same caravan. Its the last of them. We prefer to travel by lorry and car now. You can get around faster. Someone in England is interested in it."

"And what happened to Tom Ward?" she asked.

"He came to the city. But sure he could not live in the place and he was too old to take to the road again. He died six weeks ago. Had he died in the caravan we would have burned it but seeing that he died in hospital we'll sell it."

"And what of his horse?"

"Oh he is grazing along the long acre. A bit of a nuisance. The children ride him now and again but they are always getting into trouble. It looks bad to have children riding wild through the streets. We would be well shut of him."

"And does he come with the caravan?"

"He would be good riddance. But you don't look like a woman that would be intent on buying a horse and caravan ."

"Oh no. I was passing the way and I started dreaming. Just dreaming. I'd better be on my way home." And with that she emerged into the grey light of day. Her mind was still filled with ideas as she made her way home.

That night after Mrs Carney had read to the children she told them of the caravan. They were excited and planned journeys through Ireland in it, following the various roads on a map and looking at the names of the towns and the small villages. And then the dreams faded. Their mother put them into their beds and tucked them in for the night. She went downstairs to do some darning. As she was threading the needle she remembered the lottery ticket. She took it from her bag, placed it on a small table and began to rub away the silver surface with a twopenny piece. A thousand pounds, ten pounds, five pounds, five pounds, a thousand pounds. She knew that the combinations were against her and she had never been lucky. She shaved away the final square. It showed, as she suspected, ten thousand pounds. so she pushed the card aside and took up her knitting again. Then something struck her. She took up the ticket again and looked at it carefully. The final number was not ten thousand pounds but one thousand. She began to pant with excitement, her hands trembling. She had won one thousand pounds. Her first instinct was to waken the children but she managed to contain her excitement. When her mind was settled she began to think. She would pay the Shark back his three hundred pounds and be done with him. Already she had paid him two hundred pounds for the money she had borrowed.

But then a new excitement began to grow in her imagination. She thought of Tom Ward's caravan. "No," she said to herself. "Put such daft notions out of your head. You must behave in a responsible way." But she had behaved in a so-called responsible way all her life and it had only brought her misery and pain. So she returned to her thoughts, then took out the map of Ireland and looked at it. She did not look at the main roads but at the small by-roads, where there would be little traffic, where life would be slow.

Before she went to bed she again examined the lottery ticket very carefully. Yes. She had won one thousand pounds. She placed the ticket neatly in an envelope and put it in her bag. That night she did not feel the cold penetrate the thin blankets. Her imagination was on fire with wonder, and courage was growing in her heart.

2
The Decision

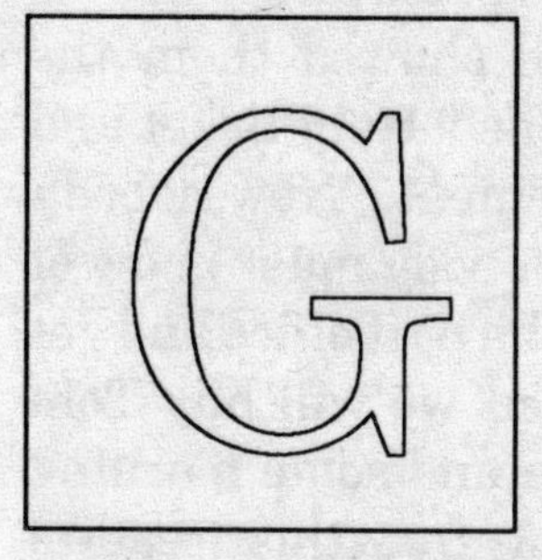

rey light poured over the estate and filled all the canyons. At eight o'clock people began to move out of the labyrinth in cars and buses. At nine o'clock children drifted towards the huge school with its four acres of cement playground. At ten o'clock there was dull silence again.

Mrs Carney waited for the children to waken. When they came down to the kitchen she had two plates of steaming porridge ready for them. It helped to keep hunger at bay. She felt guilty that they were not at school but they were so unhappy there that she sometimes let them take a day off. Several times the principal had called her to the school to ask her for an explanation. She could not understand the mother's attitude and told her that she was spoiling the children.

When Michael and Maeve had finished their breakfast she took the lottery ticket out of the envelope and said to them. “This is our ticket to freedom. We will leave this place and brush its dust from our shoes. She showed them the amount they had won on the lottery ticket and they looked at it in amazement. “Now nobody must know about this or nobody must know of our plans. But I will go to the post office and get the thousand pounds. Then we will buy Tom Ward's caravan and horse and some morning very early we will drive away from this dreadful place and we will never rest until we arrive at the sea cottage.”

Michael and Maeve could not believe that their mother could come up with such a daring plan. “But is it possible?” Maeve asked. “It is easy to have dreams at night-time when you read to us but this makes everything so different.”

“We must move very cautiously,” she replied. “Nobody must know. If the Shark got word of what we plan then we would never leave the place. He intends to keep us prisoners here. Now I must make plans with you. We must make out lists of things we need. We must have everything shipshape and sparkling.”

"But, mother, you haven't bought the caravan yet and maybe the old horse is too weak to draw it." Maeve was afraid to hope.

"I know. I know. Perhaps I am letting my imagination run riot. But first I'll buy the caravan and the horse."

Two days later Mrs Carney collected the thousand pounds at the main post office. She clutched her bag tightly when she got on the bus for home, taking the front seat on top, so that if somebody robbed her he would have to run the whole length of the bus. When she reached home she counted out the thousand pounds in twenty-pound notes and she and the children looked at the ten low piles. This paper money would buy them their freedom.

That night Mrs Carney left the house. There were lights in all the windows of the estate and here and there she noticed the colour-changes of television pictures reflected on the wall-paper. She reached the edge of the estate. Ahead lay the itinerants' camp with its lights and beyond that the darkness of the fields. She approached cautiously, fear building up within her. Halfway down the line of caravans she knocked at a door. A stout woman opened it and looked down at the figure at the bottom of the steps.

"What can I do for you at this hour of the night? Are you in bother or something. We don't have strangers calling at night."

"I came to see the owner of the caravan that's for sale. I want to buy it," she replied.

The woman looked at her. "Are you one of our own?" she asked.

"No."

"Well if you buy that caravan and people see you in it you will be marked as one of us. And what would you want with a caravan in this day and age? But come in here and have a cup of tea and talk to me about it. It's not my way to leave someone on the side of the road."

Mrs Carney mounted the stairs with reluctance. She had a fear of the itinerants. Perhaps the woman's caravan was filthy. Perhaps the woman's hands were dirty and carried germs. But it was a cosy warm place compared to her own house. There were pictures on the walls, good plates on display and delicate curtains to draw across the small windows against the night. The space was small. She sat down and the woman made a cup of tea.

"Now tell me why a settled woman would wish to buy Tom Ward's carvan? Have you lost your senses. It hasn't been on the road for four years and the wheels and the axles are rusty.

That caravan has more miles up than a car. It's bad value at any time."

It was over the cup of tea that Mrs Carney told the story of her life. The other woman listened in silence, then spoke. "It's a strange notion you have, but the caravan *could* get you across Ireland and the spring is here. It was only yesterday that I noticed the leaves coming on the trees and I took the air that has come across the flat lands of Ireland into my lungs. You would be doing a brave thing. Indeed I wish I were going with you for we never move about now. We are lodged here on the side of the roads with no decent water and no place to hang clothes. And any night we could be shifted by the guards. I went across and up and down Ireland in a caravan when I was a young girl and I have great memories of it. But I hear the sound of the van outside. I'll go with you for the deal and bring Eddie Ward down a few pounds. Don't mind the first price he asks."

Eddie Ward and his brother were dragging heavy pieces of scrap from the back of the van in the dim light and piling them on the side of the ditch. He looked up when he heard the two women approaching.

"And who have you got there, Mary Mac Donagh?"

"A woman who wants to buy the caravan," she answered.

"It's not for sale," he said, turning away from them and grasping a large oily car part. "And if it is for sale the woman couldn't put down the money for it. I want dry money and not bank drafts or cheques. I don't deal in that type of thing. And how do I know that you're not an agent from the tax people. I hear that they are about everywhere."

"Don't be ráiméising, Eddie Ward! Is the caravan for sale or not?"

"It is."

"And the horse with it, for it's not worth much to anyone without a horse. This woman here might buy a caravan, hand you good money and not have a horse to go with it."

"The horse is thrown in, though it's not far he'll take them for he is facing his last summer. I should have sold him to the knacker or the dog-food people."

Eddie Ward was in a querulous mood but the woman understood him. "We're talking around things, Eddie Ward. How much do you want for the horse and caravan?"

"Two thousand pounds," he said curtly.

She let out a loud abusive laugh. "Are you taking leave of any senses you have? Do you think you are selling a Rolls Royce or that the woman here has robbed a bank? Money is not as easy come by as it was."

"Let her make an offer. She has a tongue in her head." He turned to Mrs Carney. "How much will you give me for the lot, ma'am?"

"Five hundred pounds," Mrs Carney plucked up her courage to say. It was now Eddie Ward's turn to laugh.

"If I were to break it up and sell it for kindling I'd get more than that for it," he said.

By now a small crowd had gathered about the little group and the drama was entering its second act. The itinerant woman turned to the audience.

"Here's a woman who wants to buy old Tom Ward's caravan and make tracks to her home in the west and the bold Eddie is asking a king's ransom for it. Sure she'd get a van and a trailer for two thousand pounds!"

"It's not worth two thousand pounds or anything near it!" someone in the crowd called.

"If there's interference there'll be no deal at all. I'll come down five hundred pounds but that's as low as I'll go."

"Seven hundred pounds," Mrs Carney said.

"That wouldn't keep me in tobacco and drink for a year. It's not down in the last shower I came."

"Give it to the woman at a fair price!" someone else said.

"She's getting it at a fair price."

"She's not. At most it's worth a thousand pounds."

"I'd be giving it away for nothing for that— and a fine horse thrown in into the bargain."

"Nine hundred pounds," Mrs Carney said. "That's all I've got and that is as far as I'm prepared to go."

Both parties, the buyer and the seller, had climbed down and the audience knew that the drama was over. Eddie Ward slapped Mrs Carney's hand. "Done," he said.

And with that she took out a wad of notes and paid him in front of all the itinerants. It was a bond of trust and no papers were signed. Then she turned to Mary MacDonagh and gave her twenty pounds.

"That's luck money," she said.

The other woman was amazed at her generosity. She knew that Mrs Carney was now left with only thirty pounds. "I'll have it clean and sparkling for you when you come for it. Give me four days and it will be like new."

Mrs Carney told her the plan, that she would come on the night of the fourth day and collect the caravan and that she intended to leave the estate that same night before there was even the suggestion of dawn on the horizon. She then walked home in a high state of excitement. She had made the decision. Now she must live with it. The bargain had been sealed.

3
The Flight

he preparations for the departure were exciting. To an observer the house would have seemed quiet, but inside, Mrs Carney, Michael and Maeve carefully laid out their plans. They made long lists of all the things they would need on their journey. Things they would not need they packed into boxes, brought to the second-hand shop and sold.

Within four days they had emptied the house of everything they didn't need. At night-time they pored over a large map of Ireland. They spread it out on the floor and picked out the roads they would take and the places they would visit, planning to keep away from the main roads where the traffic was heavy. Their mother read them many travel books which stimulated their imagination. Besides the travel books they studied books of the countryside which showed them the wild life in colourful detail: the trees, the flowers and historical monuments. Ireland outside the vast labyrinth of houses was teeming with life and variety. There was no end to all the things they would see. They were eager to begin their journey.

And then one morning the Shark came. His visit was quite unexpected. Normally he arrived on the evening when the children's allowance was paid. He had an oily smile and his teeth, which he picked with a silver toothpick, looked hard and voracious.

"I've been hearing things," he began as soon as Mrs Carney opened the door.

"Like what?" she asked cautiously, wondering if he had discovered that she had won money in the lottery.

"Like your selling off furniture to the second-hand shop. Now I asked myself why should Mrs Carney sell necessary items like a table and chairs out of the house. And I began to wonder. Perhaps she is thinking of doing a midnight flit or something. But where would she go? There is no place for her to go. Perhaps she wishes to pay off her lawful debts, I thought. Now I know that you made one hundred pounds on the sale, so I've come for my money," he finished gruffly.

"I pay you ten pounds a month, you blackguard, and that's all you'll get!"

"So I'm a blackguard now. It wasn't long ago that you were on your knees for a loan. Then I was anything but a blackguard. Hand over what is rightfully mine."

"I'll give you ten pounds like I always do and you'll be satisfied with that."

The Shark pushed past her into the house and quickly went through all the rooms. They were bare. Michael and Maeve were huddled together in the kitchen. He took Maeve roughly by the shoulder and shook her. "What plans have you made? Don't lie to me," he roared. But she began to cry and he threw her aside like a rag doll. Then he turned to the boy and looked angrily at him. "You know who I am and what power I have. I could have the three of you in prison for not paying your debts."

"You could not. You are a rogue and a robber and a shark," Michael answered him defiantly.

The Shark drew out and hit him on the side of the face with the palm of his hand. It was a mistake. He became angry. He roared loudly, but this only fuelled his anger and made him irrational. Then he pounded on the kitchen table and roared again. "I'll be back every second day and every second day I'll demand ten pounds. And I'll drain you poor. Do you hear?" With that he snapped ten pounds from Mrs Carney's hand and walked out the door.

He turned at the gate. "And if you think that you can leave this estate without my noticing you are greatly mistaken. I have paid eyes everywhere."

Mrs Carney was trembling with fear when she closed the door. The two children rushed to her arms. "Mother, we will never escape now! We are cornered. He's like an Alsatian dog. He'll catch us if we make a move," cried Maeve.

They stood as if frozen together for a moment. Mrs Carney reflected on their despair. Then she had an idea. "It might work. It might just work."

"What?"

"Get everything ready. By this time tomorrow we might be out of this terrible place."

At three o'clock that afternoon, Mrs Carney left the house. She made her way to the itinerants' camp. When she saw the caravan she could not believe her eyes. It glowed with rich paint. The faded designs had been highlighted and it reminded her of her first bright vision of Tom Ward's caravan halting at the sea cottage many years ago.

Mary MacDonagh was scrubbing the floor

inside the caravan. When she saw Mrs Carney she came down the steps to her.

"It looks like new," exclaimed Mrs Carney.

Mary MacDonagh was proud of her work. "Indeed it does. Everyone in the camp gave a hand when I told them the story. The old men gave me their advice. It is waterproof and wind-proof and the floor has been sealed. Even the horse has been brushed down and washed. He is not a racer but he will draw it at a steady pace. He was bred to draw a caravan and he won't be happy until he's on the road again. His hoofs have been pared and he's well shod."

"I can never repay you for all you have done," Mrs Carney said.

"It gave the children something to do and besides they should know what it was like in the old days. Some of them can't harness a horse any more. When you live on the edge of a city where you are not wanted you lose your natural ways. You know, I feel like taking off with you," Mary MacDonagh laughed.

"That's if I ever get a chance to take off." And with that Mrs Carney told her the whole story of the Shark and how he had descended upon her and frightened the children.

"I'd have his guts for garters before I let him raise his hand to one of my children," Mary

MacDonagh said angrily.

Then Mrs Carney explained her plan.

"Now that's a brave idea! I'll make all the arrangements."

Mrs Carney made her way back through the estate to her own house. A youth in a leather jacket who lived two streets away was sitting on a wall observing her. "Don't cross the Shark," he said gruffly. "And don't leave the estate. That's a warning."

She realised that he was one of the Shark's eyes—one of the spies who were everywhere.

When she arrived home the children rushed to her. "Is everything ready?" they asked excitedly.

"As ready as it will ever be," she replied. "Is everything prepared here?"

"Yes."

"Good. Now we must wait."

Their hearts were beating rapidly. They waited.

Darkness came and the lights came on in the houses of the estate. They were fortunate that the street lights had been broken on Dargle Road and the place was in darkness except for the glow coming from front windows.

***

"Where are youse off to at this time of night?" the youth challenged the driver when the strange caravan drew level with him.

"I'm coming to collect scrap, you idiot," Eddie Ward replied.

"I'm not an idiot," the youth told him angrily.

"Your mother must have forgotten to tell you then."

"I thought youse travelled in vans these days."

"We do, but oats is cheaper than petrol and you can't beat a horse for a short journey."

"Your type are not welcome around here," the youth called abusively as Eddie Ward continued past him. The horse and caravan passed through the estate and reached Dargle Road. The youth listened to the clopping sound of the horse's shoes fading around the corner.

Mrs Carney rushed out the door when she heard the caravan approaching. Eddie Ward got down quickly and came into the house. Together they carried out several boxes and placed then in the caravan. Finally they took out the mattresses and pushed them in on top of the boxes. It took them an hour to clear out the house.

"Now, into the back and not a word from you.

One of the Shark's "eyes" as you called them, is on the lookout for me."

It was dark in the caravan and the Carneys lay on the mattresses, not daring to draw a breath. The caravan began to move forward. It was drawn slowly by the old horse and they felt that they would never find their way out of the labyrinth. They had no idea how far they had gone. But after what seemed an eternity Eddie Ward called to them.

"You are safe now. We are on the open road. The caravan is yours. It is pointing west. Light the night lanterns so that motorists will not crash into you. Keep moving towards Celbridge under cover of darkness. Keep to the small roads and always camp in a quiet place away from houses. I hope you have not forgotten how to untackle a horse."

"No. I still remember."

"Then good luck. I might run into you some day for I'm up and down the country in the van."

He got down from the caravan and handed the reins to Mrs Carney. His van was parked close by. His brother sat in the driving seat.

"You're on your own now. And luck go with you."

And then he disappeared. Quickly the Carneys took the four lanterns and lit them.

They placed two on the shafts behind the caravan and two above the door.

"We've made it! We've made it!" Michael and Maeve cried out.

"We've made a *beginning,*" their mother replied.

She gave a flip to the reins and the horse began to move into the darkness by an old instinct. They said nothing for a moment. They listened to the jangle of the harness and the crunch of the iron-rimmed wheels on the road. The air was rich with the scents of the unseen countryside and they were full of joy. Above them the heavens sparkled with stars. They called out the names of the constellations to their mother. They felt as if they were on a ship sailing across a tranquil sea. They had escaped from the labyrinth. Their mother, who had rarely spoken Irish to them while they lived on the estate, now began to sing a Connemara song. They listened to her sweet voice. Their hearts were sharp with a new happiness. Ahead lay the wide plains of Ireland and freedom.

4
The Breath of Freedom

he Carneys travelled for many hours in the darkness. Soon the traffic lessened and by three o'clock they had the countryside to themselves. Now the stars were lustrous in the skies and the air was cold. Michael and Maeve wrapped themselves in blankets. Michael sat on the narrow seat while Maeve sat in the open door. Here and there on the landscape they could see the square lights of windows, which gave them a sense of comfort.

By now their mother had gained confidence in herself and in the horse. He moved at a steady rhythmic pace. He too seemed to enjoy the travel. Michael and Maeve were so filled with excitement that they could barely talk and few words passed beween them. They were surprised at their mother's courage. The day before they had seemed to be trapped for ever in the labyrinth, but now they were freed from the long cement roads, the sameness of the houses, the small dreary patches of garden where nothing grew.

In the darkness they came to the brow of a hill. Below them lay a bowl of lights, amber and white. It looked like some mystical place, deserted by its inhabitants. They moved down the steep hill towards Lucan. Michael and Maeve gazed in awe at the silent, mysterious village when they stopped at the traffic lights and waited for them to turn green.

"Let's see the village," their mother suggested. "We are in no geat hurry and we have the whole place to ourselves. Now can you remember what you read about Lucan?" They searched their memories. Michael could remember that Patrick Sarsfield had lived there many hundred years ago, that along the river was situated the Lucan demense and that once upon a time people came to the spa to take the waters. But now the children were more interested in the present. The sound of the hoofs making an even drum-beat on the road seemed ghostly as they moved down the village. They felt that they possessed the whole world because everywhere the people were sound asleep.

They gazed at the houses fitting neatly into the streetscape, not new or brash or offensive but gentle and mellow. Then they crossed the bridge at the end and returned to the main road. They had barely spoken while they moved through the village. The big housing estate seemed many miles and many days away and the wonder of Ireland was beginning to enter their minds.

They waited at the traffic lights for a second time and when they turned green, they moved off into the inviting night. Streetlights brightened their way up the hill and out of the village. On the right was the old wall of an estate with great trees growing inside, but they couldn't make out which kind of tree in the weak orange light.

"You're the navigator, Michael," his mother said when they moved down the hill and came to a fork on the road. "Will we turn to the right or to the left?"

Michael took out the large Esso map and studied it intently under the lantern.

"We'll keep away from the main road and the heavy traffic, mother. Let's take the road on the left. It will carry us to Celbridge. We can camp there during the day and have a rest."

"Very well then. To Celbridge we will go. All

the roads of Ireland belong to us," his mother replied happily.

"It's wonderful to be away from the estate," Maeve said. "I know I'll sleep well tomorrow and I won't be screaming with nightmares."

"The Shark will never find us now," their mother murmured. The very name reminded them all of the dreadful time they had been through and how poor they had been. Now they did not feel poor any more.

The patient horse drew them through the night. Soon the landscape was dark about them again. They looked at the wonder of the heavens above them. The Milky Way was bright with a wide band of stars that glittered like diamonds. They seemed to pulse with energy. The heart of the universe was beating. In the estate the orange street lights had banished most of the lustre of the stars.

Although it was dark, they were conscious of the world about them. They knew that in the fields some fox was searching for prey, that a shy badger,with its coarse deep hairs and white striped head, was also in search of food. And all over the fields and in the woods, day-flowering plants had closed their petals against the chill of the night. The children were touched by the wonder of the dark world about them. There was so much to learn and their minds were keen. Wrapped in blankets, their faces just appearing, they looked like cowled monks in some enclosed monastery.

The old horse was very tired now and the rhythm of his steps began to grow slower. His breathing was heavy and laboured. Their pace was greatly reduced. They would have stopped but they could not find a siding in the darkness.

It was still dark when they arrived at Celbridge. The lights outlined the houses. It seemed to be a very private place. They stopped at the village green and Michael immediately climbed down. He fetched water from a pump and carried it to the horse in a pail. While he drank, Michael stroked his forehead slowly and carefully. He wished to build up a bond of trust with the animal. Then he took oats which Eddie Ward had left for him and let him feed from his hand. Michael felt the warm tongue lick on his palm. He had never touched a horse before and he was conscious of the warmth of its body and the smell of strong sweat. The animal now belonged to them and he would take care of it.

After the horse had eaten, the children went back into the caravan. Their mother drew a curtain between them. They undressed and fell asleep.

Mrs Carney sat by herself on the small seat at the door of the caravan. There was much to consider. As she reflected upon the decision she had taken she felt amazed at her courage. Some fresh sap was stirring in her body. She was like a plant which had not been watered and had been out of the sun for a very long time. She listened to the shy movements of the night: a man wheeling a bicycle along the road, passing from one amber cone of light into another and then blotted out by the darkness; a fox passing across the grass; the rustle of the wind. Her sense of smell was also sharp to the freshness of the night, the soft dampness filled with the rich scents of spring.

She wondered too if she were free of the Shark. He was there at the back of her mind—a black menacing image, the overgrown head on the large body. Even though she was protected by the darkness she felt that he knew where she was. His words rang in her ear. The Shark never abandoned his prey.

When she was troubled by such thoughts, she placed her hands around her knees, drew herself together and rocked over and back to a slow cry until she purged the image from her head. When she was at ease and the pain at the back of her head had lessened, she began to feel sleepy. She went indoors, drew the door shut, lay on a mattress and drew a blanket about her. When she awoke, light was pouring in the door, the two other mattresses beside her were empty and the curtain drawn back. The children were awake and busy outside. Michael had fed the horse and Maeve had already been to the supermarket. They harnessed the horse to the caravan and they moved away from the town before they drew too much attention to themselves. They were still shy of people and they wished to be alone, away from prying eyes.

The horse was refreshed after the night and his fondness for the countryside was returning. His eyes seemed sharper and he whinnied with delight. Eventually they came to a grassy space under chestnut trees and close to a steam. They drew in the caravan. Soon they had a fire lit in a circle of stones. Their mother fried a fine breakfast of eggs, rashers, and sausages. The rich scent of the frying filled their nostrils. When they had finished the meal they felt that a new life was beginning for them.

"I've never tasted anything more delicious except at Christmas," Maeve said.

"From now on you'll always eat such breakfasts. You'll grow strong and never suffer again from terrible winter colds. Both of you have lacked the sun for far too long. The cottage by the sea is cosy and we will never want for fuel or food."

Michael went into the caravan and found his book on nature. He wandered into a wood close by. Soon he was in the centre looking up at the dappled canopy of leaves. Down through the branches sunlight poured. It lit the pathways of the wood with magical slanted shafts. He stood transfixed. He expected some figure from the ancient Irish stories he had read to step into the fairy beams of light. He stood and gazed in silent wonder about him. So great was his delight that he felt like weeping. All this wonder had been kept from him for so long. And now it was everywhere about him. He had kept a scrapbook of pressed leaves which he had gathered in the Phoenix Park. Under a magnifying glass he had studied their neat and ordered structure. He wondered at the fine veins which fed the outer edges of the leaves. They were like a network of small canals carrying cargoes of food to and fro across the landscape of the leaves. Here all wonder began. Here the sunlight was changed into sugar and out of this came all life. Each small cell was alive with this wonder. The quiet miracle went on about him in the wood.

The spell was broken when a twig snapped behind him. He turned round. His sister had followed him. She shared his interest in nature. They began to identify the various trees from their bark, their branches and their leaves. The tree they loved most of all was the oak, with its odd angular branches, its distinctive leaves. It was old and strong and great ships had been built from the timbers of oak like this. They went further into the wood and discovered hazel trees with slender supple branches. And everywhere was the odour of old branches and trunks decaying into the floor of the forest and forming the humus for young plants. All this they had read about in their books. Now they could stretch out and feel the firm barks, rough or smooth, or bend down and crumple decaying leaves to powder in their hands.

"We'd better go back," Maeve suggested. "If we move too far into the wood we could get lost and we shouldn't leave our mother alone. She is still afraid that the Shark may come after us. It is better for us to continue our journey. If we hurry we could reach the Shannon in four days."

They went back to the caravan. By now their mother had washed the dishes and packed everything away. They climbed up and moved forward slowly. Their curious eyes could see the marks of man and nature everywhere. Cattle grazed calmly in the fields. The farmers passed them in tractors and waved to them and once they passed a school. The yard was filled with the voices of children. When they saw the caravan they rushed to the wall and looked curiously at it passing by. Michael and Maeve felt very proud.

"No school for us this month," they rejoiced as they passed the school.

"No school," their mother replied, "but you must read your books. And the whole journey will be a geography and a history lesson for you. In years to come you will remember this time more than any other time in your lives."

When they were passing through Clane, Michael flicked through his *Shell Guide to Ireland* and read out the description of the town. They discovered that there had been a monastery here and that Clongowes Wood College lay to the north-east. It was quite difficult to remember all the details from the book. Then they looked for a road sign for Prosperous. When they found it, it pointed west.

"To Prosperous we go," their mother directed. She was speaking Irish. As they moved westwards, she seemed to remember more and more of the language she had spoken as a child. It was probably because they were leaving Dublin and the Shark far behind.

5
The Shark in Pursuit

he Shark moved through the estate in his ugly horned car. It was a metal predator, moving slowly, its grilled radiator like silver teeth. It dominated the centre of the cement roads and cars drove up on to the kerb as it approached. Behind the wheel the great, glittering eyes looked out from a round and fleshy head. Beside the Shark sat Gumpus Cackle, his sidekick. He had come back from his latest disappearance looking more menacing than ever. He was small and thin, with a crooked nose and skin that was as hard and tanned as shoe leather. Many said that his blood was jaundiced and that was why his skin was yellow and dirty-looking. Gumpus was feared as much as the Shark. He moved quickly and he wore knuckledusters on his right hand. He had been to sea for so many years in flight from the law that he usually spoke in nautical terms, so his vocabulary was limited, almost monosyllabic. And he ate only fish and chips, even for his breakfast. As a result he smelt of vinegar and grease and his hands were always oily.

"All ship-shape, skipper, and in order," he said to the Shark. "Just one call to Dargle Road and we've bagged the loot for the day."

"You mean secured the interest on our investments," the Shark corrected. He wanted to make his business appear good and honest so he used banking terms.

"If you say so, skipper. If you say so," Gumpus Cackle answered, snapping closed the antique doctor's bag in which they kept the soiled and frayed money. The Shark detested the money of the poor. He loved crisp bank notes, newly-printed and with sharp images.The money of the poor had been clutched and balled in impoverished hands.It was thin and listless. Gumpus Cackle collected and counted the money, brought it to the bank and returned with new money. In this way the Shark could feel that his business was clean and respectable.

"Veer right and tack slowly," Gumpus Cackle instructed the Shark. "And we'll pay a visit to the Carney woman."

As they turned the corner The Eye gave them the nod. Everything was going smoothly. Mrs Carney was obviously at home. One call and then the Shark could return to Tumbleweed House and play pool with Gumpus Cackle. He always played pool with Gumpus Cackle because he could beat him every time. Once Gumpus Cackle had pocketed all the balls in one go and the Shark had cracked a pool cue on his skull. Gumpus had learned a severe lesson, that the Shark did not like to be beaten. He did not like people to pull fast ones on him and he always sought vengeance.

The Shark and Gumpus Cackle left the car. They made their way up the cement path to Mrs Carney's house. All along the road, eyes peered from behind curtains. They had heard the whisper that Mrs Carney had left the house with her two children. They wondered how the Shark would react to their departure.

The Shark knocked at the door and waited. Nothing happened. He knocked louder, shuffling from foot to foot. Nothing happened. He then banged at the door with his two fists, drumming his anger on to the wood. The Shark looked about to see if he was observed. He could swear that people were looking at him from behind curtains and laughing at him. Then he ordered Gumpus Cackle to break down the door. Gumpus Cackle stood back, did a small jig, let out his karate roar and charged at the door. But he bounced back and fell on the ground.

"Me bones is broke, skipper. Me bones is broke," he cried. The Shark bent down and jerked him off the ground.

"Brains is what you need in an operation like this." With his elbow the Shark smashed the front window, opened the catch from the inside and ordered Gumpus Cackle to climb through and open the door. When this was done the Shark walked into the house. He knew instantly that the place had been abandoned. He rushed from room to room. It was obvious that the Carneys had taken their meagre possessions with them.

"They have scarpered. They have scarpered!" he roared in a voice like a bull.

"But how, skipper? How? They was firmly anchored here," Gumpus Cackle cried.

"I don't know. But I intend to find out. Nobody scarpers on me. Nobody. I'll get to the bottom of this before I get to the top. Let's see what The Eye has to say. He'd better come up with a good answer."

The Shark stormed from the house, followed

by Gumpus Cackle. They got into the car and screeched down the road, leaving angry tire tracks on the cement.

The Eye was waiting for them at his section of the estate. Before he knew what was happening, Gumpus Cackle had jumped from the car, caught him by the leather jerkin and hauled him into the back seat of the car. When he had gathered the few wits he possessed, he was looking at a brass knuckleduster.

"Talk!" Gumpus Cackle said.

"What about?" The Eye asked.

"Geography," the Shark said.

"I was never no good at geography in school," The Eye said. "I don't even know where London is."

"Not *that* Geography, you eejit. Where are the Carney woman and her children?" Gumpus Cackle asked, printing the brass knuckles on The Eye's jaw.

"They never left the road. Never," he whinged.

"Think—or you'll have a feed of teeth. Something must have happened," Gumpus Cackle said.

"I'm thinking," he cried. He thought hard—a difficult thing for him to do. "They never left the place. They are still there. "

"Soften him up, Gumpus. The Eye is not too bright today. People don't drag mattresses past The Eye without The Eye seeing. They must have hired a van."

A sharp knuckle jab into The Eye's ribs made him scream for mercy. He was desperate to answer the Shark's questions. "Nobody entered or left the estate except Ward from the camping site," he cried.

"Ah! The Eye is beginning to remember. Tell us about Ward."

"He was gathering scrap."

"When?"

"At night."

"Seems a strange time to gather scrap."

"He said it was something to do with tax and that hay was cheaper than petrol."

"And you believed him? You saw nothing wrong with his story," the Shark remarked sarcastically.

"No. Not at the time."

"You blind eejit. Even Gumpus could explain what happened. Tell him what happened."

"Sure. Ward was out exercising the horse and no better place to exercise the horse than here," Gumpus Cackle replied.

"I have two eejits in the car instead of one. The Carneys were in the caravan. Now why

Ward should help them escape from my grip is something I have not yet figured out. But I'm going to and I'm going to do it right now. Get rid of that eejit," the Shark ordered.

The Eye was thrown on to the pavement. The car sped away. The Shark was angry and when the Shark was angry he was inclined to do rash things.

He sped dangerously through the estate. Dogs scampered from the road and cars drew aside. Soon he arrived at the encampment. He drew up sharply, got out of the car and made straight for Eddie Ward.

"I want to talk to you," he roared.

"Maybe I don't want to talk to you," Eddie Ward answered in a hard voice.

"If I want you to talk you'll talk," the Shark roared louder.

His voice carried across the encampment. Men, women and children began to take a hostile interest in the Shark. They had heard about his rough practices. They moved towards his large figure and the small figure beside him.

"Easy with your tongue. Easy with your tongue, skipper. There's a gale force brewing. Watch out for squalls," Gumpus Cackle cautioned.

"I don't like either you or your voice. You've

brought a rotten stink into the camp. We'll need a barrel of Jeyes Fluid to get rid of it," said Eddie Ward.

"I wash myself twice every day. I spray deodorant under my armpits and after-shave on my neck," the Shark replied.

"A Shark will always smell of shark," said Eddie Ward. The Shark hated the name Shark. He drew out to hit the itinerant but Eddie Ward grasped his hand and slowly bent him to his knees.

"Use your knuckleduster, Gumpus," the Shark screamed in pain. But Gumpus Cackle had grasped the situation around him and did not move.

"I'll pay for information. I'll pay for information," the Shark cried. By now he was on his knees on the damp ground.

"If I see you near this place ever again, I'll rub your nose in the dirt. Do you hear?" Eddie Ward told him.

"I do."

"And do you understand?"

"I do."

"Out loud."

"I do."

"Good. Now get into that stupid car of yours and get out of my sight."

By this time the whole camp was in an angry mood and the men had to be restrained by their wives. The Shark and Gumpus Cackle rushed to the car, followed by a shower of eggs, which were mostly rotten. They left the estate spattered with stinking yellow yolk.

"I'll be back. I'll get even. I'll buy a bulldozer and doze them out of the place," the Shark roared. As he passed back through the estate people began to laugh at the car and the two occupants. This had never happened before. The Shark felt that his dignity had been diminished. He must recover his power.

He passed through the great gates of Tumbleweed House in a fury, rushed out of his car and went directly to his room. He showered for twenty minutes, then sprayed under his armpits and rubbed after-shave into his neck. When he returned to the drawing-room he still smelled the egg from Gumpus Cackle.

"Get out of my sight, you evil-smelling little shrimp. Go outside and wash yourself down with the hose and don't come in here until you smell properly," he shouted. He felt he was tainted all over again and he took another shower. He sprayed deodorant under his armpits and rubbed after-shave lotion into his neck and returned to the drawing room in a cowboy suit. He always did his best revenge-thinking in a cowboy suit. He did not feel ridiculous.

When Gumpus Cackle returned from the yard where he had washed himself, the Shark was sitting in his large cowhide chair chewing tobacco, a nasty habit he had picked up from cowboy films. He was deep in thought.

"You know something, pardner? I been a-doing some thinking," the Shark said in a cowboy drawl. And you know what, pardner?"

"What?" Gumpus Cackle asked.

"I think I got me some answers. Yes siree! I got me some answers."

" And what are the answers, skipper?"

"Why I believe that little old widder woman and her two mites have gone and purchased them a caravan and are heading out west."

"Going to Californier to them there green hills," Gumpus Cackle said in a drawl, trying to humour the Shark.

"No, you eejit," The Shark said, jumping up and throwing aside his cowboy hat and his cowboy talk. They purchased that caravan or hired it and headed west towards Athlone."

"Oh you mean *that* west."

"*That* west—the west that is signposted by the county council. We must go after them."

"And will we go now?"

"Right away. I think that we should track them before nightfall. "

***

Gumpus Cackle was not a lover of the country. Nature to him lay in city streets and city buildings, pool halls, betting shops, garages and supermarkets. Trees were to burn, fields were green wastes and rivers barriers which had to be bridged. He did not enjoy the notion that they should go into the country even if it were only for a day.

It was evening when they set out. They had packed some things into a bag and a suitcase. The Shark drove viciously along the green-banked road and soon they were in Lucan. Thinking that his reputation was known in Lucan, he parked his car on a double yellow line outside the post office. He was about to lock the car when a voice behind him spoke. "Who do you think you are? Do you see the yellow lines? You're blocking the entrance," a sturdy postman said.

"Do you know who I am?" the Shark asked.

"I don't know and I don't want to know," he replied.

The Shark was about to argue with the postman when a guard approached. "What's the problem, James?" he asked the postman.

"This individual is blocking the entrance to the post office."

The guard studied the Shark carefully. "Aren't you that well known blackguard from Dublin. Be on your way with you before I take your name," he ordered sternly. "And take that leprechaun with you," he said, pointing to Gumpus Cackle.

The Shark and Gumpus Cackle were having a bad day. The firm authority they held in the estate did not work in the country. The Shark was about to respond with a smart remark but Gumpus Cackle said, "Be careful, skipper. Hold your temper, skipper."

They parked further down the road and then returned to the main street. They found a bar and the Shark ordered himself a drink. He looked about him at the faces of those who were sipping pints and staring morosely at their reflections in the long pub mirror.

"Did anyone happen to see a caravan passing through Lucan some days ago?" he asked the line of faces. They remained silent.

"A round of drinks for the men," he ordered. Their faces became alive. They began to talk.

"Was it a yellow caravan?" one asked.

"I don't know."

"Well if it was a yellow caravan it did not pass through Lucan."

The Shark was irritated. Clearly he could not obtain proper information. He paid for the drinks and they left the bar. His anger was at boiling-point.

"We'll go further," he said.

They passed down the road to Leixlip and sought further information. Nobody had seen any horse-drawn caravan. The Shark was frustrated. He took out his map and began to study it. The whole place was netted with roads that led everywhere and anywhere. He scratched his head.

"I think we'd better give up the chase, skipper. Let them go," Gumpus Cackle advised.

"I'll not give up. They have to be somewhere," the Shark replied, stabbing crossly at the map. "I'll find them. We'll return home and resume the search tomorrow. I have to think."

"Very well, skipper. Very well," Gumpus Crackle said, delighted to be returning to Dublin.

It was late when they returned to Tumbleweed. The Shark watched a cowboy film and then went to bed. It had been a frustrating day and he was angry.

6
The Midlands

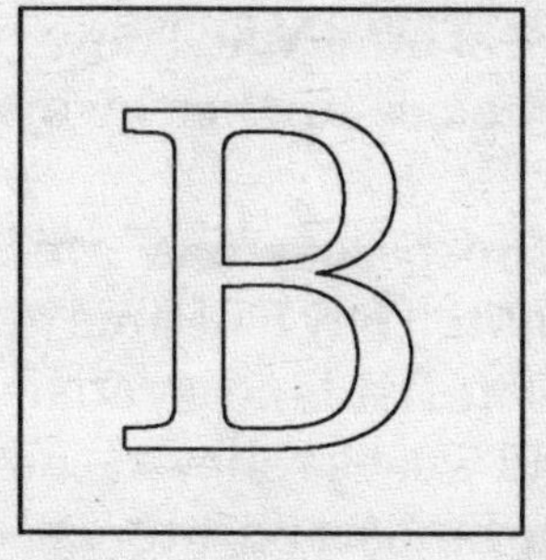

y now the Carneys had become familiar with the caravan and the horse. The animal had improved in every way since he left Dublin. His eyes were brighter; there was a bright sheen on his coat and his breathing was free. He ate the green grass with relish and Michael fed him with oats every morning before they started out. Now the Carneys knew that they could do twenty-five miles a day in the caravan. With luck they would reach Galway in seven or eight days, but they were in no great hurry. There was so much of Ireland to see and they knew that they would never have the opportunity to make the journey again in quite this way. And they preferred the small by-roads. The traffic was not dense there and they had a sense of a green Ireland. They could never get used to their new-found freedom. Once, during the night, Maeve had jumped up in the bed screaming, "The Shark, the Shark! He's at the door!"

But her mother soothed her. "No, the Shark is far away. We are well free of him. You'll never see him again. Each day we are further away from him."

They passed through Prosperous and continued on towards Rathangan. They had time to take in the flat midlands. The flat land stretched to the horizon. Trees and woods relieved the wide expanse and made the landscape interesting.

Spring was almost at an end. The leaves had not yet turned fully green and the small woods were filled with inviting mystery. In the fields the grass was beginning to thicken. Easy clouds passed across the sky casting moving shadows. Nothing could now dilute the childrens' pleasure. The whole countryside was like a vast library. They plucked the flowers and found their names in an old book, by a botanist named Thomas Fox, which their mother had bought in a second-hand bookshop. It was frayed and torn but they did not mind. Magic and wonder was everywhere. The nights of study in the cold and bleak house were now showing fruit.

Early one evening they reached Monasterevin. They drew the caravan on to a wide grassy margin. All of them were now quite expert at untackling the horse. Soon he was grazing contentedly while Mrs Carney set about making an evening meal. The children had collected some small branches in a wood and soon food was frying on the pan. Maeve and Michael loved the rich aroma. When the food was prepared the three Carneys ate a filling meal. Later they had time to explore the town. It was a pleasant place, small and tidy, situated where the main road to the west crosses the River Barrow and the Grand Canal. As they looked at the quiet canal they pictured the wide barges with their cargoes moving through the heart of Ireland from Dublin in the age before the railways and the motorcars.

Maeve and Michael knew that to the south of the town lay Moore Abbey where John McCormack had lived for many years. Their father had owned a collection of his records. They were old seventy-eights, much scratched by use. But the clear far-away voice of the great tenor had always given pleasure to their father. He told them how McCormack was born at Athlone and how he had conquered the great opera houses of the world. And he never tired of saying, "John McCormack had the greatest voice ever given to man since Adam. Now that's something to remember and to be proud of."

They could recall the voice of their father as he sang the songs about the house. That night as they stopped overnight so close to Moore Abbey, their mother sang some of their father's favourite songs for them. The songs were haunting and the night made them seem sadder than they actually were. The children's hearts were full of painful joy and they hoped that their journey through Ireland would last for ever.

***

It was on the flat road to Clonaslee that they met the Fiddler for the first time. He was a tall, thin man. His clothes were loose because he was so thin and he wore a wide-brimmed hat that suggested that he was an artist. He had a red scarf knotted under his chin. His face was weatherbeaten from travelling up and down the roads of Ireland, but his eyes had an arresting brilliance. He shambled along with his fiddle case slung across his back. When he saw the Carneys, he doffed his large theatrical hat and bowed. "A good and a musical day to you, fellow travellers on the roads of Ireland."

"And a very very good day to you," Mrs Carney answered. She had stopped the caravan.

The Fiddler examined it carefully. "Yes, it's a fine caravan. And well painted too. Don't see too many well painted caravans anymore."

He examined it more carefully, stooping down to look at the ornamental work on the wheels and on the shafts. Then he went around to the back arch of the caravan and examined that too. "Something tells me that this belonged to old Tom Ward," he said with professional pride. "Once upon a time I knew every caravan that travelled the roads of Ireland. But now I never see them except abandoned and falling to pieces."

"You're right. It did belong to Tom Ward," Mrs Carney replied. "You have a good eye for such things."

"A good eye and a good ear," he told her, pointing to his fiddle case. "And where, may I ask, are you going?"

"To Clonaslee and by way of Clonaslee to Galway."

"And may I presume to ask you why you travel west in such a vehicle. Why not take a train or a bus?" he inquired.

"It's a long story!" she said.

"I have all the time in the world to listen to a long story. May I sit up on the seat and go with you for a ride. My feet are tired."

"But you are coming from Clonaslee!" Michael reminded him.

"And now I'm returning to Clonaslee. I have no fixed time for anything. I can follow my whim and I have a whim now to return to Clonaslee and go on further with you if you would be gracious enough to give Frederick the Fiddler a ride." His language sounded dramatic and as he talked he acted out his words with his hands.

Mrs Carney invited him to take a seat. The children sat at the door, fascinated by the tall fiddler with the artistic hat.

"And now tell me *your* story," he said.

As they travelled along the road to Clonaslee they told him their story. Each one took a turn in telling it. Frederick the Fiddler listened with close attention to everything that had happened to them during the previous weeks. When they were finished he commented, "A most extraordinary story. It would well fill a book, and a fascinating book at that. The Shark certainly sounds a large nasty fellow and his aide, Gumpus Cackle, a small nasty fellow. Not people you would wish to meet on a dark night or on a bright day. But all that is well behind you and you are truly knights of the road. I shall now take my fiddle and play for you, for I always believe in paying my way."

He opened his battered case and took out a fiddle. It was a lustrous brown and they were all surprised by its beauty and finish. It was without scratch or blemish.

"Did you ever hear of Antonio Stradivari?" he began.

Michael and Maeve were surprised by his question. "No," they answered.

"Well let me tell you about Antonio Stradivari." As he tuned his fiddle he spoke of the great man from Cremona who had made the finest fiddles in the world.

"And this is one of them. If you look inside the scroll you will see the great man's name on ancient paper."

"But why do you not sell it? You could be a rich man!" Michael asked.

"Sell it? Sell it? I *am* a rich man. And every one who hears one of my tunes becomes richer in his heart although he may not realise it," he answered with a certain amount of annoyance. "I cannot be bought."

He touched the strings lightly with his thumb to test their tone. "Now what would you like to hear? I play jigs and reels on it but for you

I will play some light and airy thing by Johann Sebastian Bach. You know something about Bach?" he asked before he began.

"No," the children said.

"Oh, there is much for you to learn. Did you know that his wife used some of his music paper to line her cake tins? So we have lost some immortal music."

"What is immortal music?" Maeve asked.

"Music that will last for ever. When the pop songs of today are forgotten, the music of Bach will still be remembered." He took his fiddle and placed it beneath his chin. Taking the bow, he drew it across the four strings and listened to their sound. Satisfied that they were in tune, he began to play. It was a a sprightly piece of music and it was played on the way to Clonaslee in the Midlands. It had a light and delightful quality and even the horse seemed to take joy in it.

"Now that's Johann Sebastian Bach for you, played on a Stradivarius," Frederick said when he was finished. He was about to place the precious fiddle in the case when Mrs Carney asked him to play some more. He needed little encouragement. All the way to Clonaslee and from there on to Kinnitty he played.

Then he replaced his fiddle in its case and he began to tell the family stories of his travels through Ireland. He was one of the most interesting men they had ever met in their lives and they did not feel the day pass.

They halted outside Kinnitty. Mrs Carney invited Frederick the Fiddler to join them for their supper. He accepted the invitation. "But first let bring some offerings to the feast," he suggested. "I shall be gone for some time, so expect me when you see me."

He disappeared into a nearby wood. Michael and Maeve also went into the wood and gathered some dry branches. Soon they had a merry fire burning in a circle of stones. The children sat gazing into its warm heart. They were so taken by its wonder that they did not talk for a long time. They were warm and comfortable and the mystery of the countryside possessed them. An hour later the Fiddler returned with four trout. They were gutted and ready for the pan.

"Sometimes I earn my supper and sometimes I catch it," he said. "I have learned to live off the land and that's a good thing. Modern folk don't know how to do this any more. I found some field herbs to give the fish a fine taste."

He laid the fish neatly on the pan, shredded some of the herbs, placed them on the trout and watched them simmer.

When the trout were ready they all ate them. They were like no fish they had ever tasted before. They had the subtle tang of the branches and the herbs and the flesh was brittle and dry. They sat about the fire and watched it die. When the fire collapsed into glowing embers the Fiddler left them. They pleaded with him to stay but he said that he must move. He took his fiddle case and disappeared into the darkness. They thought that they would not see him again. But he was soon to return with very disturbing news.

7
Hate

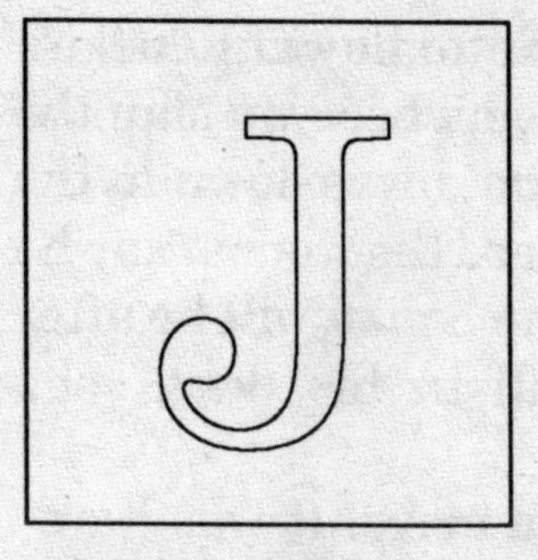

ohn Derrick was a large fat slob of a man. His heavy eyes, set above pockets of flesh, seemed perpetually wet and the lids were sticky with mucus. He wore loose clothes which were old and greasy. There was no reason why they should have been old and greasy because he was a rich man. But like his wife, who was thin and as tall as himself, he was a miser. He loved money and he loved looking at it. Night after night he would take out the tin biscuit boxes which contained his wads of dirty notes and he would count the notes. "We'll go over it again, Kate, just to make sure that we have the whole ten thousand," he would say with pleasure.

Sitting in front of the wood fire they would lay out the dirty notes and count them together, in greedy harmony. "Nine thousand, nine hundred and ninety eight, nine thousand, nine hundred and ninety nine, ten thousand!" and their voices would be as loud as voices at a football match when a goal was scored.

"With that you'll be able to buy O Rourke's land. Won't he be surprised when you slap the money down in front of him. I was down in the village yesterday and I heard the women say he was on a right scatter. The banks will be after him any day now to call in his debt," she chuckled.

"And then we'll make a move. It was hard-earned money, Kate, put together pound by pound. Better in the biscuit boxes than in the bank, for the fewer who know your business the better."

"If it were ever stolen what would we do?" his wife asked.

"I don't know what I'd do at all at all. It would be the death of me. But it won't happen, Kate. I'll guard it and you'll guard it and I'm thinking of buying an Alsatian to guard it when we are out."

They hid the boxes under the stairs during the day and at night-time they carried them to bed. They ate well. She kept poultry in a large shed they had bought from the army. They were free range hens because she was too mean to buy them feed so she let them forage for themselves about the yard. They never grew tired of eggs because they did not have to buy them and every third Sunday their table was graced with the remains of old hens that were past laying.

Kate Derrick was never without the poor mouth. When she went to the village shop, she wore an old faded red coat and decaying hat that she had bought in the 1960s. Her back was bent with worry. She loved giving out about the priest, the teachers, the politicans and the guards. "Oh it's well for them. A secure job and sure of the cheque at the end of every month. Not like the rest of us scraping and scrimping. Ah the times are hard and from what I can read in the paper they are going to get harder. Things are going from bad to worse. But sure I have to keep going and my health is not that great." And when she finished her speech she always gave a rough cough.

"This cough will be the death of me," she told the villagers, who were used to her performance. Even the children could imitate her.

The burglary must have happened the evening of Pat Kiely's funeral. John Derrick had no great regard for Pat Kiely but both he and his wife visited the farm to pay their respects. He wanted to take a look at the condition of the Kiely land and his tractor. Pat Kiely's would be coming up for auction and if he failed to secure O'Rourke's land, well Kiely's would do just as well.

The thief was almost caught in the act. He had moved quickly about the house looking for the money. He knew that it had been secured somewhere. And then just when the Derricks were returning, he discovered one of the boxes under the stairs. With nimble fingers he prised off the lid, grabbed the money and placed it in his pocket. He replaced the lid, slid out the back window and disappeared across the fields in the gathering darkness. He was a professional and left no traces.

"They could have given us a drink instead of cups of tea and buns. Oh the relations aren't going to waste a penny on him. That was the cheapest coffin I ever saw in my life," John Derrick complained as he poured the tea, which had been brewing for three hours on the range, into his mug.

"I thought that Deignan's coffin was just as cheap," said his wife.

"I don't believe it. But I had a good look at the tractor. It looks worse than it is and they might knock it down for a hundred pounds. I could do a job on it and sell it for a hundred profit. That way we'd have gained something from the evening."

They drank the tea and considered the events of the day.

"I think it's time to count the money, Kate," John Derrick reminded his wife, and he fetched the five biscuit boxes from beneath the stairs and placed them on the table.

"Soon it will be invested in good land," he boasted, as he lifted the lid of the first box, took out the money and placed it on the table. It was when he opened the fourth box and plunged his hand inside that he realised that something was wrong. He searched around with his fingers. He held up the box to the light to see if had been holed. He shook it but no money fell out. He turned pale and then purple. His heart began pounding.

He began to stutter. "We've been rob-b-b-bed."

"What do you mean?"

"Look for yourself."

"Are you sure the money didn't fall out underneath the stairs?"

They took a bicycle lamp and rushed to the stairs. They searched about and pawed empty potato bags aside to see if the missing money had fallen among them. But they found nothing. They returned to the table like two robots, they sat down like two robots and were without feeling like two robots.

Then John Derrick let out a roar that frightened the hens. "It's the itinerants. They're behind it! They're behind everything!" He grabbed his double-barrelled shotgun and loaded it, thumbing in the cartridges in anger.

"I'll shoot them. They'll not rob a decent man," he called to his wife. His face was purple and she was afraid that he might have a heart attack.

"Take it easy. You can't go out in the dark. You should tell the guards."

"And they'd inform the taxman and I'd have to pay two thousand pounds more on what I have left. No. I'll have to figure this out for myself. I'll go into Birr and see if there are any itinerants about the place."

He set off for Birr, having decided to visit several of the pubs and discover as much as he could about the movements of itinerants. But everyone knew his form and nobody paid him much attention. He went into the hotel, acutely conscious of his shabby clothes, made his way to the bar and sat on an oak stool. He looked at the man beside him, a stranger with a sharp intelligent face. John Derrick looked at his fine fingers and thought that he might be a gentleman. The man looked up in surpise when John Derrick sat beside him, but all he said was, "May I have the pleasure of buying you a drink?"

"Well fair dues to you sir! I'll have a double whiskey," Derrick replied.

The stranger ordered the measure of whiskey and paid for it in dirty pound notes. Then he paid for a further round.

"You're a generous man and I can see by your face you are educated. We'll here's to you," said Derrick as he threw back the second free whiskey in one gulp. It went to his head and soon he began to tell the stranger of the tragedy which had befallen him.

"I'm a broken man tonight, sir. A broken man. Hard earned money gone and some blackguard of an intinerant is drinking it at this moment. There's no justice."

The stranger seemed anxious to get away. He ordered John Derrick another drink and paid again with filthy pound notes. Then he excused himself. "I must get on to Galway. I have to deliver a lecture at the university," he explained.

"On what?"

"Micro-cellular statistics as applied to the interior structure of molecular combines."

"Anything to do with cattle or tractors?"

"I'm afraid not."

"Well I wouldn't be interested in it, then."

"I must be on my way."

And with that the stranger left the lounge. He slipped out the back door carrying a black suitcase, got into his car and sped off towards Dublin.

"There's one decent gentleman," John Derrick said to himself as he left. "He bought me three large whiskeys. There's nobody else in town who would buy John Derrick three large whiskeys."

He made his way home drunkenly in his car. The next day he vowed he would track down the itinerants who had stolen his money.

***

Next morning the Carney family set off for Birr. They were coming closer to the majestic Shannon. Once they had crossed the bridge at Portumna the sea would be only two or three days away. Time was passing so quickly for them. Sometimes they felt that they should veer south and cross the Shannon at Limerick.

In that way they would have passed through the whole heartland of Ireland. But they were anxious to get to the sea, anxious to take advantage of their good fortune.

Each day the heavy burden that had weighed so heavily upon them seemed to lighten. But soon an incident occurred which frightened them and gave them a sharp insight into the lives of the itinerants. It happened on the road to Birr. They stopped by the side of the road to have a meal. By now each of them had become very professional at making fires. Michael had gathered some dry branches and broken them across his knee. He put them on the small fire of kindlings and they were soon caught by the updraft of flames. They crackled noisily and broke. Soon the fire was glowing with a deep heart. Michael placed an iron tripod over the fire and suspended a pot from it. It was a warm day, still and full of fresh scents. Maeve was feeding the horse with handfuls of oats. Her mother had begun to use Irish phrases and Maeve was eager to learn all the new words she could from her mother so she called to her and asked her the word for oats. "Coirce," her mother answered with a smile. Maeve saw that she was happier now than she had every been before. Her face glowed, she had more energy and the worry lines seemed to have disappeared from her forehead.

Soon she had a midday meal ready for them and they sat about the fire eating from white plates. Suddenly a man burst through the hedge beside them. He wore a greasy tweed hat and a donkey jacket. His heavy face was round like a pudding and netted with purple veins. He carried a double-barrelled shotgun in his hand and his wellingtons were heavy with mud as if he had been walking through wet fields.

"I'll not have you near my land. If I had my way I'd have you breaking stones," he roared, moving forward and pushing the tripod into the fire. He pointed the gun directly at them and for a moment the children feared that he would pull the trigger. His face showed primitive anger and he acted without thought. He did not give the Carneys time to rise but continued in his rage.

"Thieves. I know you. Filthy and unwashed. Well you are not welcome in these parts so be on your way before I let you have it with this." By now the children and their mother had gathered their wits. They looked at the pot turned sideways on the blazing fire, the contents boiling out into the flames.

Mrs Carney was angry at this brutal man

who had burst in upon their peace but she had endured too much from the Shark to be frightened by him. The children watched in fear as she stood up and walked toward him.

He pointed the gun at her. "Did you hear me?" he shouted, the gun shaking in his hand. "I said be off with you this moment. The likes of you are not wanted here. You never did an honest day's work in your lives. Living off the rest of us you are. If I had my way I'd pack you off out of the country."

He glared at them and then moved towards the door of the caravan. "Where were you yesterday?" he demanded, poking his head in at the door.

"Are you threatening me?" Mrs Carney replied firmly.

"Yes, I am. I've set your type scampering with a good blast of my gun before."

"You're a brave fellow behind that gun,a big fat bully. I'm a citizen of this country. I have a right to be here and you have no right to threaten me with a gun."

"Be off, I tell you. I'll have no back-chat from a tinker's wife. I'm looking for something that belongs to me. It was stolen by your lot and I'll not rest until I find it."

"Are you certain that 'our lot,' as you call

them, stole your belongings?" she asked.

"Who else could it be? Aren't you behind every robbery between here and Athlone?" The gun was still quivering in his hand.

"Be careful with that gun," she warned. "It might go off and do us harm."

"I'll not take orders from a tinker's wife."

"They are not orders. They are directions," she commented acidly.

The argument might have darkened had not a squad car passed that way. The guard stopped the car and came towards them. "What is the cause of this bother, Derrick?" he asked.

Before the man could say a word, Mrs Carney moved towards the guard. "I wish to press charges against this man," she said. "He has abused me and my children, he has threatened us with a gun and he has destroyed some of my property."

The guard was taken aback. He was surprised at the manner in which the woman spoke. "Are you sure you wish to press charges?" he asked.

"Yes, quite certain. The man is a coward and a bully and threatens defenceless people," she replied in her fine accent.

By now John Derrick was speechless with rage. Very few people stood up to his threatening presence. Finally he managed to speak. "You don't believe her, do you guard? Would you take the word of a tinker's wife against that of John Derrick. Law and order are breaking down. I never thought I'd live to see the day. I don't know what the country is coming to at all."

"The children are witnesses. You did threaten us with a gun beside a public highway. I know my rights," Mrs Carney insisted.

"You have no rights," John Derrick shouted.

The guard decided that he must act. He was impressed by this woman who possessed both dignity and intelligence. "If she presses charges, then you will have to appear in court. What is your name?" he asked.

"Well enough you know my name!"

"What is your name?" the guard asked again.

"John Derrick."

The guard took more details and then closed his black notebook. "You'll be hearing from me. You've been warned about this behaviour before," he said sternly.

"I'll get even with them! I'll get even with them," John Derrick promised as he moved off, shaking his fist.

The guard waited until Mrs Carney, Michael and Maeve had collected their things and stored them in the caravan. Then he saw them safely out of the area.

The Carneys were badly shaken by the incident but they continued their journey.

8
Birds of a Feather

eanwhile in Tumbleweed House, the Shark had composed himself. He realised that he had acted rashly. He should have been more cautious: he should not have attacked Eddie Ward and he should have been more polite at Lucan.

"Don't tell me, Gumpus Cackle! Don't tell me I made a mistake. I know I did. But there will be no mistakes any more. We will move swifty. I have looked at the map and I know where we are going. Straight down the main road. Then we'll cut down to Birr at Athlone. Somebody is bound to have seen them at one of these towns. They'll not escape from me, mark my words!"

By now the news that Mrs Carney had escaped the clutches of the Shark had circulated the estate. Some people in the estate, who had been watching the Shark's operations, now found the courage to move against him. They had already gone to the police station and reported some of his crimes. And once the first witnesses came forward others began to follow. The move against the Shark was building up like a flood pushing against a river bank.

But the Shark was unaware of all this. He was obsessed by his desire for vengeance. He would set out early in the morning and comb the Midlands in search of a horse-drawn caravan driven by a woman and two children.

"I think we should give it a miss, skipper. The Midlands are far away; foreign seas, you might say, with dangerous reefs," Gumpus Cackle advised the Shark. He had cleaned the gaudy car and polished it and the Shark cast a sharp eye over it. He had on a wide-brimmed hat and his bulky coat, trimmed with fur. It was expensive and bought with money wrested from the poor. It made him look even larger, like a circus ring-master.

"To the Midlands we go, Gumpus. The whole business should be cleared up in a single day. I'll squeeze them for the last penny they have and then I'll come back for more." He squeezed his hand into a tight ball to show that he was determined to honour this threat.

"OK, skipper, if you say so. Should I bring a suitcase of clothes?" Gumpus Cackle asked.

"No need to. We'll be home before night. Mark my words."

Gumpus Cackle had no wish to cross the Shark. He got into the gaudy black car with the steers horns. The Shark with some awkward ceremony got in behind the wheel, started the car, banged the door and off they went in the direction of the Midlands.

Dublin flew past and Lucan and Maynooth and Kinnegad and Tyrrellspass and Moate and then they were in Athlone, the town that straddles the Shannon. The Shark, who had had a meagre breakfast, went to the best hotel and ordered a large and early dinner. Gumpus Cackle bought fish and chips which he had to eat outside the window of the hotel. Inside the Shark tucked into his dinner, which consisted of many courses and included a bottle of wine and a large chicken which he savaged and hacked with a knife. It must be said of Gumpus Cackle that he was a nimble eater and was dainty in every gesture. He nibbled at his chips and he ate only small morsels of fish. When he was finished he bundled the paper and put it in a *bruscar* barrel.

"I feel fine now. Just fine," the Shark said,

patting his stomach as he emerged from the hotel. "But I must sleep." So he locked himself in the car and fell into a long after-dinner sleep. The jowls of his face blew up like balloons as he snored until Gumpus thought that they might burst.

"And no harm if they did," he said to himself, standing outside the car and looking in. "I don't like the smell of the Midlands. I wish I was in Dublin."

When the Shark had had his sleep he pawed his face and exercised his jaws. He was wide awake now. He opened the door and Gumpus Cackle sat in. "We'll go to the bar closest to the river. If a caravan passed by, that is where we should hear about it. These people always have their eyes on the street. And let me do the talking. All you have to do is cry. Do you hear?"

"Cry? But I haven't cried in years," Gumpus replied, surprised at the command.

"Well you're going to cry now. If necessary you will weep streams of tears. The Liffey won't be in it with you!"

"Give me a reason why I should cry?" Gumpus demanded in protest.

"Because if you don't, you'll find yourself stranded in the Midlands like Robinson Crusoe and secondly you are weeping for your sister and her two children who have gone missing in a caravan. Understood?"

"Yes, skipper."

They found a pub close to the main bridge. The Shark went in, followed by a tearful Gumpus Cackle who sat in a corner and began to cry and call out, "Where are they, where are they? Gone and left me. Gone and left me."

He was very loud and the Shark had to restrain him. He went to the bar. The old lady, portly and soft-faced, who was serving behind the bar, looked at Gumpus Cackle huddled over his tears in the corner.

"Is your friend coming from a funeral or something?" she asked the Shark.

"Oh, indeed no. It's not quite as bad as that. His sister and her two children left him in Dublin and they came west in a caravan and he's broken-hearted without them. Broken-hearted!"

"I can see that," she said, drying a glass and looking sympathetically at the little man in the corner. "It's a sad world."

"And did you see a caravan pass across the bridge by any chance?" the Shark asked.

"Well indeed no. I'm always seeing big lorries passing across the bridge but if a caravan passed I'd definitely see it. Wouldn't I, Pat?" she asked one of the regulars who sat with his elbows on the bar.

"Mrs Boyle misses nothing. Better than the guards she is. Didn't she see two bank robbers going across the bridge one day right under the guards' eyes. Amn't I right, Mrs Boyle?"

"That's right, Pat."

"And you got your photograph on the local papers. Amn't I right, Mrs Boyle?"

"That's right Pat."

"And you got a reward. Amn't I right Mrs Boyle?"

"That's right, Pat."

The Shark was beginning to lose his grip on his good manners and Gumpus Cackle was wailing like a banshee in the corner. "So no caravan passed?" he asked.

"No," said Mrs Boyle.

"If it had, Mrs Boyle would have seen it," Pat added. "Do you remember the time you saw Jim Figgerty passing and the whole country looking for him?"

"That's right, Pat."

It was too much for the Shark. Valuable time was being lost. He rushed down to the corner, caught Gumpus Cackle by the ear and dragged him on to the road.

"Wasn't I good enough?" Gumpus asked in

pain.

"Too good. We must hurry. We'll head for Birr."

They started out for Birr, which lay to the south and beyond the towns of Ferbane and Cloghan. A few miles outside Athlone, Gumpus began to turn pale.

"What's wrong with you, you eejit?" the Shark asked.

"I'm seasick. It's the grass that does it to me."

"Well, don't be seasick in this car. If you are, I'll leave you marooned in the Midlands like Robinson Crusoe—as I said before."

On the road to Ferbane the front tyre burst. They skidded into the ditch and a horn was wrenched from the front of the car. They got out of the car and took stock of the damage.

"I still say we should have stayed in Dublin. There's a bad black eye on us and we'll come to no good," Gumpus Cackle complained.

"We'll need a crane to get the car out of the ditch," the Shark said. He surveyed their lonely position. They were in desperate need of help. "Start crying," he ordered.

For the second time that day Gumpus Cackle started to cry. Soon a car stopped and the Shark explained that Gumpus Cackle was on his way to see a very sick relative. He must get to a garage in Ferbane. The kind stranger gave Gumpus Cackle a lift to Ferbane while the Shark sat in the car.

Eventually the car was hoisted from the ditch by a small crane. The Shark reluctantly paid the garage owner. He and Gumpus left the wretched place with one horn sticking from the bonnet of the car. Finally, at nightfall, they arrived at Birr. They drove around for some time before they discovered a small squalid pub which had a good view of the road.

"Start crying," the Shark said as they were entering the pub.

"I've no tears left," Gumpus Cackle answered.

"Invent them," the Shark ordered.

Gumpus Cackle entered the pub crying. It was a dreary ill-lit place with few customers, among them John Derrick and Frederick the Fiddler.

The wailing of Gumpus Cackle soon filled the small bar.

"Can you get that fellow to shut up?" John Derrick answered. "What's wrong with him?"

"It's bad," the Shark began. "He's looking for his sister and her two children. They came through Birr in a horse-drawn caravan. He misses them something terrible."

John Derrick jumped from his stool. "He's another one of them," he roared. "A bad day they came through the town."

He ran down the bar and caught Gumpus Cackle by the neck. He would have strangled him had the Shark not pulled him away.

"If I had my gun, if I had my gun!" Derrick roared.

"Stop roaring," commanded the Shark. "There might be a few pounds in it for you if you give us information. Sit down."

"What do you mean?" Derrick asked sourly.

"I'll tell you what I mean." They sat in a corner and the Shark began to talk in whispers.

Frederick the Fiddler pretended that he was asleep in a corner close by. He began to snore lightly. But he listened carefully to the conversation of the three men in the corner. It was marked by threatening words. They were determined to make the Carney family suffer. Frederick the Fiddler was quick to realise that the big man with the expensive coat was the Shark, who had held the family in terror for so long.

"It's too late to catch up with them now. Come the morning I'll go with you. There is no road between here and the Shannon that I do not know. Mark my words, we'll catch them early in the morning. There's no place where they can run now. They are cornered," said John Derrick malevolently.

"I'll only be certain of that when I see it with my own two eyes," said the Shark. "They slipped past me once and I won't let them slip past me again."

He unfolded a large map of Ireland and looked at it. He examined the network of roads. If the Carneys intended to cross the Shannon it would have to be at the bridge to Portumna. There was no other way for them to reach Connacht.

"Even if they do cross, we'll get them," he promised.

Later, Frederick the Fiddler pretended to snort awake. He cleared his eyes and looked about him. He rose from his seat, took his fiddle case and left the room. The street was lit by a few isolated lamps. He felt almost helpless as he looked towards the road which led to the bridge over the Shannon. Even if he spent the whole night looking for the Carneys he must find them. They were in deadly danger.

He began to walk west. If he could get them safely across the Shannon there were farms where they could hide for a while and never be noticed. He had many friends on the west bank of the river. He walked into the night. The road was lonely and dark but he had sharp eyes and he knew the way well. He walked faster.

9
Wide Waters

he Fiddler was six hours on the road before he found the Carneys. It was still quite dark. They were camped up a side road and it was only the smell of burning wood from a dying fire that led him to them.

They were asleep when he knocked at the caravan door. "Who's there?" Mrs Carney called.

"The Fiddler. Get dressed, I have bad news for you," he called to them.

Soon they were all dressed. They emerged from the caravan, still caught up in sleep. "What's wrong?" the mother asked.

"The Shark. I saw him in Birr. He is with an evil-looking ugly small fellow and now they have joined company with a heavy loutish farmer who bellows and roars and calls for his gun. He seems to believe that all problems can be solved with a gun."

"The small man is Gumpus Cackle and the man who has joined them sounds like the farmer who threatened us today. He is a nasty creature with little regard for people's rights. He believes that we are itinerants," Michael said.

"Well, they expect to catch up with you very soon. So we must move out of here. There's no time to waste."

"And where shall we go? We cannot reach the bridge in time. They'll have us cut off by morning," Mrs Carney said anxiously.

"We will move north towards Meelick. There are some side roads where we can hide. But we must hurry and get away from the main road. Main roads are dangerous. If we can cross the Shannon, then I know places where we can hide out. I have many friends along the way. We must get to the Connacht side of the river," said the Fiddler.

There was much confusion in the darkness until one of the caravan lights was lit. The horse was harnessed and the utensils gathered up from about the smouldering fire. The lamps were secured and then they moved forward into the night, knowing that they had a safe hour of darkness before the dawn. They passed down small roads, where trees stood like spectres on each side. Very soon the countryside began to be visible in the grey light. An hour later it was almost bright. They still moved along narrow country lanes, continually looking behind to see if the Shark was coming. All their old fears had returned and they thought now only of their safety. There was no way in which they could reach a bridge over the Shannon and they would have to hide somewhere. Then they came to the end of a small lane and there in front of them flowed the great river. It was like a wide and deep moat around Connacht. They looked at the fields on the far side and wished they were there. Mrs Carney brought the caravan to a halt on a cement slipway which was used for launching small fishing boats.

All they could do now was wait. The children were terrified when they thought of the Shark and his friends.

It was the end of spring and the very beginning of summer. Even the mornings had some heat and the night dew was quickly dispersed. The river brightened under the light of the sky.

"I think we should eat," said Frederick the Fiddler.

"But how could you think of eating at such a

time?" Maeve asked, her heart filled with anxiety.

"It will take our mind off things and anyway, it is better to be fortified with a good meal. Besides, what better place to have it than on the banks of the Shannon," the Fiddler replied. "We'll start a fire and I'll do the cooking for a change so your mother can relax."

Maeve set about gathering small dry branches which the Fiddler placed in a cone. He set a match to the dry grass at the centre and soon aromatic smoke began to rise from the heart of the fire. When it was blazing he set stones about it, took the black pan and began to prepare the breakfast. The smell of cooking gave them all appetites and soon they were eating heartily. However, they could not put the thought of the Shark and his friends out of their minds.

***

That same morning the Shark had a large breakfast before he set out on what he took to be the last leg of his journey. He was drawing in the ends of the net and no escape was possible. Soon he would return to Dublin and resume his wicked ways. He ate alone at the hotel. He lived well and he ate well and when he was very hungry he ordered two breakfasts, as he did on this occasion. The country air had given him a hearty appetite. When he was finished, he brushed the breadcrumbs from his clothes, wiped his lips on the table napkin, let out a sigh of pleasure and wished that he was beginning his breakfast all over again. Having settled his account he set out to meet his companions. Gumpus Cackle had slept in a shed and was stiff and cold. John Derrick had returned home, counted his remaining money, gone to bed and told his wife Kate that he was off the next day to catch some thieves. He came back to meet the Shark and Gumpus early in the morning. They all got into the Shark's car and the Shark described the two breakfasts he had just eaten.

"Well I'm still hungry, skipper, and not a fish and chip shop open," complained Gumpus Cackle.

"You know that it is ill-mannered to talk about food like that," said the Shark.

"It's all right for you with your stomach filled. I'll faint if I don't get a feed of fish and chips," Gumpus Cackle replied, a hint of rebellion in his voice.

"It's back in the nick you'll be if I hear another word from you," the Shark warned him.

Gumpus Cackle fell silent. Anger burned in

his mean heart. He looked out the window of the car at the summer morning but it was of no interest to him and stirred no response in his mind.

"I think it will be a fair year for bullocks," John Derrick observed. "You can tell by the growth in the fields."

But the other two had no interest in agriculture. They were eager to finish up their business in the Midlands and get back to the city. They headed straight for the bridge over the Shannon. They waited there for an hour but no caravan appeared. Then they called at some houses along the way and asked the owners if they had seen a caravan passing along the road. But nobody had seen anything. It became evident to them that the caravan was still on the Leinster side of the river.

"Now we will scour every side-road until we get them, for they have to be hiding somewhere," John Derrick told them. "I know every corner and cranny and every by-way."

With the detailed map spread out before them they began the final part of the hunt. They searched along every small road in a meticulous manner. Now there only remained the few side-roads leading to the banks of the Shannon. One by one the roads were covered until finally they turned into the small road to the slipway.

There in front of them lay the caravan. Sitting around a small fire they saw the Carney family and a strange-looking man. They had caught their prey. The Fiddler had placed some stones across the road so they could not drive directly to where the caravan was stopped. The three men parked the car, threw open the doors and moved towards the little group around the fire.

Mrs Carney gazed in fear at the approaching figures. Her flight from Dublin had been futile. Here at the very centre of Ireland the Shark would be able to gloat over her misery. He would take the caravan from them and leave them abandoned on the bank of the great river.

It was at that moment of greatest fear that she made her decision. It seemed reckless but it was born out of necessity. "Into the caravan!" she shouted. "If the Shark wants his money then he'll have to swim for it."

"But will the caravan float, Mother?" the amazed children asked.

"We can only try. I will turn if we begin to sink. Hurry. We haven't a moment to lose."

"It's a long way across," the Fiddler said, looking at the far bank which now seemed a great distance away. The dark waters flowed between them and safety. Towards the centre the current was fast and dangerous.

"And it's a long way to Dublin and I have no intention of ever returning there again," Mrs Carney replied between clenched teeth.

She urged the horse forward. Slowly he pulled the caravan down the corrugated slipway. It began to roll towards the water. Excitement gripped the children, an excitement greater than their fear. They were proud of their mother. Ever since she left Dublin, courage and confidence seemed to have grown within her.

"Now I want the two of you to plug any leak you find. Tear up a sheet. I hope that the floor is well leaded. It is important to bale out out the water as quickly as possible," Mrs Carney told Michael and Maeve.

The horse continued down towards the water. The Shark looked on as the caravan slid down into the Shannon. The wheels slowly sank into the water.

"They will surely drown," John Derrick shouted. "It will be good riddance to them. Good riddance. If only I had my gun I'd give them a blast."

For a moment the Shark thought that the wooden caravan would sink. But then to his surprise it began to float like a barrel. It moved out into the current and then was slowly taken downstream.

"They'll never make it! They must sink! They must sink!" the Shark cackled.

Mrs Carney held her breath. She felt the caravan taken by the water. "It's floating! It's floating!" she cried. "Watch for the leaks."

Now she kept her eyes on the brave horse tugging his burden forward, his head safely above water. His eyes were staring wildly and she called out encouraging words to him. The far bank still seemed far away and some water was pouring in at the side. It was the single weakness that could bring them to ruin. The Fiddler plugged the slit with a blanket. Then he lay against it. Michael had to look for other leaks but he could find none. The caravan had been well sealed by the travellers. The Fiddler pressed against the blanket, which was now saturated. He dared not look out the door. He could see Mrs Carney at the front, her body tight with tension, the reins in her hand. He was conscious that there was movement forward and movement downward. He hoped that a floor board would not spring.

Now the caravan was in mid-stream and moving quickly downriver. The far bank seemed to be moving further away. Mrs Carney could measure how quickly they were slipping downstream. She hoped that they would not be smashed against a bridge.

She urged the horse forwards out of the wide sweep of river. "Oh but you are the good horse," she cried. "There are pastures by the sea where you can rest if you can make this one great effort. Just one great effort and we will all be safe."

He seemed to understand her words. He moved forward and the tug of the river became less strong. And then there was no tug at all. They touched bottom in a small bay. Slowly the horse drew them up on to a sandy shore.

"Oh we've done it!" the children cried. "We've done it! " And they jumped out of the caravan and hugged the wet horse. They put their arms about his neck and cried.

"You're a brave woman, a brave woman," the Fiddler said to Mrs Carney. "No one will ever believe what you have done."

She trembled when she considered the decision she had taken. She did not know whether it had been brave or rash on her part. She had reached Connacht and her determination was now firm that she would bring the caravan and the children safe to the cottage by the sea.

10
A Time to Rest

ll at once the Carneys heard the sound of a jeep coming towards them. They looked up and saw four men dressed in tweed coats and wearing tweed hats. Fishing rods swayed above the jeep like aerials. One man had a video camera trained on the caravan.

"Are you safe, lady?" an American voice asked.

"Yes," replied Mrs Carney.

"Well let me introduce myself. I'm Jim Donaghue from America and these are some of my friends. We were just settling into a morning's fishing when we saw you drive into the river. Lucky we had our video camera. We captured the whole action. You must have some story to tell, lady. Could I interview you? We're from an American television company and we're taking in some fishing while we're in Ireland."

"Its a long story," she began.

"I got all day to listen..."

He was big, comfortable and reassuring and he wore a leather belt with a silver buckle.

Mrs Carney told her story very simply, as all the Americans gathered round to listen. Frequently she looked over her shoulder at the far side of the river, fearing that the Shark might be peering at her through the sedges.

"Are you still afraid?" Jim Donaghue asked.

"I can't shake off the fear. I don't believe that I'll ever be free of that terrible man."

"Never fear, you've got friends. We'll see you all the way to your home in the west."

It was an offer that was both welcome and unwelcome. Mrs Carney was a woman who did not wish to draw attention to herself and at the same time she needed the protection the Americans could offer. They were eager to follow the story.

"You say this Shark is bleeding other poor people in Dublin?" Jim Donaghue inquired.

"Yes, but they're afraid to speak out against him. They have no protection. People tremble when he appears. Children cry when they hear his name. He believes in force and he lives by force and he has a gang of roughs collected about him who do his bidding."

"Are you willing to say all this on camera?" Jim asked.

Mrs Carney hesitated. "May I speak to my friend for a moment?"

She drew the Fiddler aside and asked him for his advice. He did not hesitate. "You may not want the publicity but it'll give you protection. Above all it will expose the Shark."

"If it will expose evil and set things right then I'll do it. I feel that I now have courage which I did not possess before."

She went back to Jim and told him her decision.

"Good. Now let us set it all up. He has been trying to catch you, so now let us set a trap for him instead. He is sure to follow the caravan. You must hurry away from here. We have to collect our equipment from the hotel and that will buy time. When he does have his confrontation with you we must make sure it happens in Galway City, when you are not much more than a day's journey from your home. Leave it to us. It is what we are best at. You must get away from this exposed position."

The horse had now found his wind. Everyone helped to push the caravan on to the small road by turning the wheel spokes and they continued until they reached a main road. The Americans promised to join them as soon as they could.

Now the Carneys and Frederick the Fiddler were alone again. They had time to reflect on all that had happened so quickly. They were in Connacht and they felt that they could now make it to Galway.

"I know this country," Frederick told Mrs Carney. "There are so many by-ways that we could lead them a merry chase. They have had their hour, now let us have ours. I know a number of farms hidden among the small hills where we can stay for the night."

"But we would be imposing ourselves upon the farming people," said Mrs Carney.

"Not at all. Many of these people are fine musicians and when I arrive at their door I am welcomed. Before you know it, word has spread about the countryside and every musician in the district arrives for a session. I have enjoyed many a fine night in these parts."

"Couldn't we stay at a house like that, mother?" Maeve asked. "You have often told us about them and how you enjoyed the music when you were young."

"I'd feel like a beggar," said the mother.

"But for the moment we are—beggars, I

mean," Michael reminded her.

They all began to laugh. Mrs Carney drove the caravan along the road. Suddenly, it seemed, summer was in the air. The sun was warm and the fields looked greener than they had when the Carneys had started out. The hedgerows were thickening and the land looked fertile.

They felt happy now. The children were proud of their mother. Had she not taken that brave step they would have been trapped by the Shark.

***

The Shark and his two friends had watched in surprise as the caravan moved out into the swollen waters. At every moment they expected it to sink beneath the surface. But this did not happen. As if by magic it floated downwards and across. Gumpus Cackle was impressed by the manner in which it moved. He said so but the Shark knocked him on the head.

"I'm more determined than ever to catch them now. They were lucky, plain lucky, but their luck has run out. Back to the car. We must continue the search. They returned to the car and made their way back on to a minor road and from there to a major road and finally they came to the bridge over the Shannon. Here they stopped and the Shark examined the map again. Everywhere roads branched out in all directions. The net was open and he did not know how he was going to close it. He pointed to Laurencetown on the map.

"We'll go to Laurencetown. It's at the centre of everything," he directed. They set out for Laurencetown.

But now the terrain favoured Mrs Carney. As the Shark travelled north the caravan moved directly west through Ballycrossaun and then to Killimor.

The Americans had by now caught up with the caravan, having returned with their jeep and another car. "We have decided to visit my good friend, Donal Flaherty," said the fiddler to them. "Why don't you come with us? You'll be sure to experience genuine Irish hospitality. His house is very secluded and you could do your interview there."

It sounded like an excellent idea, and so the cavalcade moved on. About an hour later they turned down a narrow lane between hills and continued along for a half mile. Finally they came around a bend and before them lay a lake. At the centre was an island with fine feathery trees growing on it. About the lake's edge strange sedges grew and, tied at a small pier, floated a blue boat. Up from the lake and tucked into a hollow in the hill stood the house of Donal Flaherty.

He was waiting for them when they arrived in front of the house. He was a tall thin man, with laughter in his eyes and an Adam's apple which never seemed to rest. He took off his cap and scratched his head and looked at the caravan, the jeep and the car. "Is it some sort of invasion?" he asked laughingly.

"It is," Frederick the Fiddler said, "and they expect hospitality. But let me introduce everyone here."

While they were being introduced the cameraman was recording the event. He also recorded the welcome extended by Mrs Flaherty and her three children.

"What we have is yours," Mrs Flaherty told them simply.

They went into the kitchen and Mrs Flaherty rushed about finding chairs for everybody.

"Let me help you," Mrs Carney offered.

"Not at all. Sit where you are. You've come a long way."

It was only later, while they were drinking cups of tea, that Mrs Carney had the opportunity to tell the company about all their adventures.

"It's an unbelievable story," Donal Flaherty remarked when it was ended.

"It is a story that has not ended yet, for we are still pursued by the Shark," Mrs Carney reminded them.

"We will soon discover where he is. I think we can lead him up and down a few roads before we are finished with him," the Fiddler laughed.

In the meantime, the Flaherty children had invited Michael and Maeve to explore the farm. It was an interesting place with many historical remains. They wished especially to show them a souterrain which their father had discovered by accident three years previously. John, the eldest of the children, had brought a torch with him. They reached an old rath, with bent hawthorn bushes growing on the sloping banks. Hidden close to the ditch lay a stone opening.

"Careful," John warned. "The roof is very low and you will have to crawl several yards before you reach the hidden chamber."

Their sense of adventure banished the Carneys' fear. They dropped through the stone opening and found themselves in a dark tunnel built of great slabs of stone. They pressed forward, calling to each other, and soon they were standing in a large circular chamber.

"It's built into the mound but we have no idea what it was for. It was hardly a place to hide. We found some animal bones and pottery here. They're in the museum now."

It was an eerie place. They stood silent, listening to their heartbeats. "It would be a dreadful place in which to be trapped," whispered Michael. "There's no way of escaping."

Maeve became frightened so they pushed back along the passage again and soon they were outside. Next they visited the remains of a Norman keep. It was a thick-walled watch-tower with a stone stairway spiralling up through the centre. The keep stood on a hill which gave a panoramic view of the surrounding countryside. It was dangerous in places. But they moved up through the centre of the tower, counting out the ninety eight steps. Soon they stood on top. As they looked west they could see the town of Loughrea, with its church steeples dominating the skyline. To the south were the Slieve Aughty Mountains, rising gently out of the limestone plains. To the east lay the tranquil waters of Lough Derg.

"We crossed that big river," said Michael to the Flaherty children. "It was the most exciting and dangerous moment in my life. I'll never forget it."

The five children stood on the tower for what seemed a long time gazing at the great spread of countryside below them. Galway seemed a wide and immense county. For Michael and Maeve it was a revelation. They had been cooped up in the city for so long that they had no idea that the world could be such a beautiful and open place. They feasted their eyes on all that lay beneath them.

"I could spend a summer here exploring the countryside," Maeve told Lucy Flaherty, the youngest of the Flaherty children.

"Then why not visit us later in the year?" Lucy invited.

"And what would your mother say?"

"She would love to have you. You could sleep in my room. We have plenty of space."

The Carney children could barely cope with the new sights, sounds and scents of the countryside. Their minds were fresh and alive and everything was filled with interest. But perhaps the most exciting hour was the one spent on the lake. John and his brother Patrick were expert oarsmen. As soon as everybody was seated they punted the boat out into deep water. Then, setting the oars in the rowlocks, they rowed the boat gracefully across to the island. It was a small, mysterious place. A monk called Aidan, had once built himself a small cell at its centre and during the Penal times, a priest had hidden there.

Evening was falling when the children were finished with their excursion. They had not eaten for several hours and suddenly they felt hungry. Luckily there was a fine meal ready for them in the kitchen when they got back to the house and when they were finished eating, Michael went and helped John and Patrick milk the cows. As he stood in the barn and listened to the suction of the milking machines and smelt the animals, Michael knew that he belonged in the country and not in the city. He loved the small farm hidden among the hills, with all its historical remains and its lake.

When the boys arrived back in the house the first musician had arrived. Already news had spread across the townland and they expected several visitors before the nightfall, including the storyteller Seamus Fada. The fire crackled with wood and turf and people were sitting around the walls. There was quiet talk at first but soon a player took out his flute and played a reel. Frederick the Fiddler took out his fiddle and joined in. The night had begun.

The American television crew had interviewed Mrs Carney much earlier in the evening and now they had set up their camera in the kitchen to record the night's entertainment. They had forgotten for a while about their fishing trip and had entered fully into the spirit of the evening.

Michael and Maeve Carney would never forget that night. It was in the Flaherty kitchen that they discovered their roots. They listened to the lively reels and the sweet laments. At one moment their hearts were dancing along, the next they were filled with sorrow. They had never experienced such wonderful feelings before.

But they were most pleased when their mother sang for the company in Irish. They had not heard her sing before in this fashion. Her voice was strong and full and she seemed to have got younger. Her face was free of the tight lines which had once marked it but the grey hair reminded them of all the trouble and sorrow she had been through. The night ended with Seamus Fada telling a ghost story. The whole company stayed silent as he spun the story with the magic of his voice. He seemed to invite ghosts and spectres into the kitchen. And then when it was at an end, he clapped his hands loudly and they all jumped.

It was very late when the Carney children went to sleep and the sun was pouring its rays in the door of the caravan when they woke.

11
Tangled Roads

he Shark was by now weary and sore. He had met two Americans who had sent him in the wrong direction. He had ended up in the centre of a vast brown bog, where the wind cried and lonely birds stood by the side of dark pools. He had passed through small villages whose names he could not pronounce and now Gumpus Cackle was complaining. John Derrick had left them at the village of Kylebrack and returned to the neighbourhood of Birr. He felt he had travelled too far from his native place.

The Shark reached Ballydavid. He looked about the village. He was not pleased at what he saw. He preferred large estates with amber lighting, with streets of houses which went on and on. Villages began abruptly and ended just as abruptly.

"I need a drink," said the Shark to Gumpus Cackle.

"And so do I," responded Gumpus Cackle.

"Well if you do you'll pay for it. I'm tired of carrying you on my expense account. You have been no help to me at all. I'm losing money on this venture and I don't feel generous at this particular moment in time," the Shark said with a low growl.

They went into one of the village pubs. A few men sat at the counter, their backs to the strangers. They looked at their half-full pint glasses.

"A large whiskey," ordered the Shark. He sat sullenly by himself and looked at his drink. He seemed out of place in his large coat and his large hat.

"Do you belong to the circus?" one of the locals asked.

The Shark's eyes flared in anger. "I'm a financier," he told them. "I deal in money."

"And I'm President of America," the local man answered derisively.

The Shark was going to lose his temper but Gumpus Cackle jumped up and prevented a fight. "I'll play you in a game of pool, skipper," he suggested.

"Set up the table," the Shark ordered. My nerves are on edge and it might cool them down."

Gumpus Cackle was growing weary of the Shark and his adventures. He was homesick and he had been humiliated on so many occas-ions. Now he planned a small revenge. " What do ya say to a bet of a fiver? It will make it interesting."

"Very well. Put your money where your mouth is," the Shark responded. Gumpus Cackle put a five-pound note on the counter and the Shark covered it.

The game began. Gumpus Cackle played cautiously, but just when the Shark thought he had won, Gumpus Cackle pocketed the final ball.

It was a narrow victory.

"It was a fluke. I'll double the bet," said the Shark.

"Very well, skipper." The game began and Gumpus Cackle again edged towards a narrow victory. The Shark never suspected that his sidekick was leading him on.

When the Shark had lost three hundred pounds he called a halt. "That's enough," he told Gumpus Cackle. "I'm out of form and the table is faulty."

"Can I buy you a drink, skipper?"

"I'll buy my own, you git," the Shark answered. But when he searched through his pockets he found that he had no money left.

"Very well," he said gloomily. "I'll have a double whiskey."

Gumpus Cackle was generous with the Shark's money. He bought everybody in the bar two rounds of drinks, which made him quite popular.

"I suppose none of yez saw a caravan passing?" he asked.

"With children and a woman?" the barman said.

"Yes. The very one. The very one."

"Saw it half an hour ago west of Loughrea."

The Shark and Gumpus Cackle tossed back their drinks and headed for the car.

"That should lead them well astray," said the barman to his friends and customers. "They are two notorious blackguards from Dublin. I had a phone call from Donal Flaherty an hour ago to warn me of their presence in the area. They are up to no good, let me tell you."

Just before they got into the car, the Shark suddenly caught Gumpus Cackle by the ear. "You dirty little razzler. You dirty little razzler. You took my money under false pretences. Give it back to me."

Gumpus Cackle silently handed back the money. He was getting tired of the Shark and his ways.

The Shark and Gumpus travelled through the night. They passed through Loughrea. They searched all the side-roads but they could not find the caravan. Exhausted, they returned to Loughrea. While the Shark slept in the best hotel, Gumpus Cackle again slept in the car.

***

Next morning, after eating a good breakfast, the Shark and his sidekick set out again. They took the road east and spent the day asking questions in bars and following false trails. Finally Gumpus Cackle had enough. He was too far from home. That night he had to sleep in a hayshed outside Killimor while the Shark spent the night in a guesthouse. Gumpus believed that the fish and chips had deteriorated all the way from Dublin and when he was once offered a fish without brown batter and upon a plate he felt ill. He had seen too many green fields; he had been in too many bogs and he had visited more miserable villages than he believed existed. So next morning, with hayseed sticking to his clothes, he rebelled.

"I've had enough. I'm abandoning ship. I'm taking the homeward bound for Dublin. Give me the fare and we'll call it a day," he said, refusing to get into the car.

"I'll abandon you here, you imp. No money will you get from me. On your way—and may you end up in a bog hole!" The Shark slammed the car door and drove away, leaving Gumpus Cackle marooned like Robinson Crusoe, in the centre of Killimor.

Gumpus took out a nautical compass and looked at it. The needle pointed to the north. To the east lay Dublin. He began his journey home.

It was at this moment that fortune favoured him. A large car pulled up on the roadside.

"Are you a friend of the Shark?" an American voice asked.

"Was," Grumpus said curtly.

"Good. Would you be interested in making some good money?"

" What have I to do?"

"Talk."

"About whom?"

"The Shark."

Gumpus Cackle agreed to talk to the Americans. They set up a camera on the side of the road and he was interviewed for television. He took to the camera and poured out his heart to it. By the time he was finished he had given away most of the Shark's secrets. He even demonstrated the use of knuckle-dusters for the camera, cutting up into centre focus with a vicious blow and a cutting twist. He took his money when the interview was finished and set off for Dublin. He had decided then and there to return to the sea, where at least he would know where he stood and perhaps be actually happy.

By now the Shark, alone and angry, made his way along the small threads of roads. His temper was as frayed, but his determination to catch the Carneys was as firm as ever. He wondered again where he could obtain definite information. As he passed a small old, limestone school situated many miles from any town, he hit upon an idea. He turned his car and went back to the school. He decided that he would pay a visit to the children and the teacher. It was a long time since he had been to school but the Shark could be a good actor when he wanted. He straightened his hat and his coat and he got out of his car. One of the children, a boy called Patrick, who had been arranging books on the window ledge, saw the stranger arrive in the yard.

"It's an inspector," he called to the teacher,

who had a grey beard and grey hair. He was standing before a huge chart which held all history, as he often said to the children. It covered the whole northern wall of the damp schoolroom and was illustrated in a splendid fashion.

"There's no peace in this world. No peace at all," he told the children. They were gathered in a wide crescent around the great chart of all known history. They waited for the knock on the door. There was a tap on the door. It opened. In walked the Shark. He had on a serious face. The children stood up and called out.

"*Fáilte romhat, a chigire!*" The Shark was taken aback. But he recognised the word *cigire* because he had once had to deal with a tax inspector.

"Sit down children," he said "I am delighted to see you all looking so well. You are all well no doubt?"

"Yes, cigire."

"Good. And I presume the teacher is well too?" he asked the children.

"Yes, cigire."

The teacher became suspicious. Inspectors came in all shapes and sizes but this one seemed very much out of the ordinary.

The Shark was only good at one thing. He

was a master of arithmetic. He could add and take away, multiply and divide faster than any crook in Dublin. He began to ask the children questions in arithmetic. They answered readily.

"You are certainly the best class in Ireland," he praised them. "And now I would like to do some geography. Let me see now..." he began to think. "Who can name all the towns between Dublin and Galway?" he asked. There was a pause. They looked at the teacher. His face was blank.

"London," one answered.

"No, London is down in Kerry," the Shark told them.

"London is in England," one of the children replied. The Shark was taken aback.

"There is also a London in Kerry," he asserted, which was news to the teacher with the grey beard and the grey hair.

The children succeeded in remembering some of the towns between Dublin and Galway. The Shark praised them for their knowledge.

"And now I want you to give me the bones of a composition," he said, going to the blackboard and taking a stick of chalk. "The title of the composition is 'The Caravan'—and he wrote 'karvan' on the board.

"Cigire, cigire," one of the children called.

"What?" the Shark asked.

"That's the wrong way to spell caravan," the child told him.

" Ah! We have got an intelligent child in our midst. I deliberately spelt it wrong. Now we shall let this bright child go to the board and spell the word correctly."

The pupil, beaming at his own importance, went to the board, cleaned off the mistake and spelt the word correctly. "You may stay where you are and write down the rest of the bones. Now, did any of you ever see a caravan with two children and a woman driving through this countryside? Would that not be a good idea for our composition?" There was a sly smile on his face as he looked at the faces of the children standing about him.

"It's the Shark!" the children roared. "After him!"

The Shark was taken by surprise. He ran from the classroom, holding his big hat on his head. The children followed him like a swarm of bees. They threw their lunches after him as he rushed towards the car. Quickly he drove off down the road, his coat stained with egg, ham and jam.

"Children these days! No control whatsoever. And I intended to give them the rest of the day off," he muttered to himself.

The Shark was very confused as he made his way along unmarked roads. Meanwhile back at the school, order had returned. The teacher with the grey beard and the grey hair asked the children about the Shark. Their parents had told them to be on the look out for him. News of his presence had spread across the locality during the previous evening.

***

That very day, as the Shark wandered about the network of country roads, Mrs Carney, Maeve and Michael, with help from the Fiddler, tackled the caravan and said goodbye to Donal Flaherty and his family who stood at the door and waved them off. Michael and Maeve stood at the back window of the caravan and watched the house disappear. Then they came forward and sat beside their mother and Frederick the Fiddler.

"Yesterday was the greatest day of my life," Maeve said.

"And last night was the geatest night in *my* life," Michael added in order not to be outdone.

"You shall have many such days and nights,"

their mother promised.

They left the tangle of small roads and reached the main road leading to Loughrea. The great worry which had weighed so heavily upon them had now lifted. They felt as light and as free as the summer wind. They knew that the Shark might still follow them and the Americans hoped he would, but now they were well protected. Mrs Carney recalled the sad evenings in Dublin when they had drawn the curtains on their poverty and their sadness. She would never be poor or unhappy again. Her confidence had returned. Ahead lay the cathedral town of Loughrea. Michael flicked through his *Shell Guide to Ireland* and discovered all about the town. He read out the entry to the others.

"We must visit the cathedral," he said.

"Very well," said their mother, "we have some time on our hands."

The exterior of the cathedral was dull but when they went inside, their eyes were filled with the glory and wonder of the stained-glass windows. They looked in awe as the summer light was changed into a thousand colours. It fell in great magical pools on the floor. They moved quietly through the church and prayed before the great altar. Mrs Carney prayed in

Irish, thanking God for the safe journey and seeking further protection.

Outside it was a warm summer's day. She took the children and Frederick to a restaurant and invited them to order whatever they wished.

"Bangers and mash," cried the children in unison.

"Some things never change," laughed their mother.

While they ate their dinner, the Fiddler told them of a secluded farm where they could safely camp for the night.

"It is a calling house and I am always welcome there. It would be not be wise to travel immediately to Galway. The horse is old and he needs a rest."

"When we reach the sea pastures," Mrs Carney said, "he can rest for ever. He is a good and noble horse and he has shown great courage."

The Carneys left the town and took the road for Galway. The pace was now much slower. The horse was weary. He had walked a long way and now his old muscles were sore.

The Fiddler directed them to the small farm. It lay some distance from the road and was surrounded by trees. The night was quiet. The travellers visited the house and the Fiddler played many of his tunes for the company, but the Carneys were tired and they went to bed early. In the morning after breakfast they set off on the last leg of their journey. They passed through Oranmore and turned right for Galway.

"Look at the sea! Look at the sea!" their mother pointed excitedly towards the west.

The sea caught the morning light. The waves sparkled and shimmered and the tangled seaweed which bearded the rocks smelt strong and salty. Seagulls wheeled and cried above them. "We've made it. We have made it. Now we can truly say that we have travelled across Ireland," Maeve cried.

"Let us hurry to the Saturday market!" cried Mrs Carney. "There we shall meet all our friends, for there's no place like Galway on a Saturday afternoon."

Michael was as usual searching through his *Shell Guide to Ireland*. He began to read for the others. They listened to every word. He gave them the rich details of the historic city towards which they were then moving.

At this stage the American television crew had reached a crucial point in their programme. They had split up into two groups. One group now followed the caravan into Galway, with the camera covering the progress of the Carney family. The second part of the team was on its way to Loughrea with polaroid photographs. They kept in contact through radio phone. The Shark was not aware that he was about to be set up. The American team believed that with precise planning they could bring the whole affair to a dramatic conclusion at St Nicholas's Church.

"It is a matter of exact timing," they told each other over the phone.

They reached Loughrea. It took them only a little time to discover the Shark's Mercedes parked outside a pub. Inside, the Shark sat at the bar in a pool of confusion. Nothing had gone right for him during the last few days. He felt scruffy and in need of a bath. There was stubble on his jowls and his face looked strained. He badly needed to change his striped shirt. He felt sweaty and uncomfortable. He was about to give up the chase when fortune finally favoured him.

Two Americans came into the bar and sat beside him. They were very enthusiastic about their trip to Galway. The had seen the Cliffs of Moher, they had kissed the Blarney Stone and they had had a medieval banquet at Bunratty

Castle.

"And this very morning, I got the cutest photograph of an Irish caravan you ever saw. Ain't these two kids cute with their Mamma?" he said, and handed his friend the photograph.

The other American was in raptures at the "cute" photograph. "Don't you think that's one of the prettiest snaps you have ever seen?" he said to the Shark, who was sitting beside them. The Shark looked at the photograph. The Carney family were smiling out at him from the door of the carvan. Luck had finally favoured him!

"When did you take this photograph?" he asked quickly.

"Some two, three hours ago," the American told him.

"Where?" the Shark asked.

"On the road to Galway. To the west of Oranmore, I believe. Are you interested in taking a photograph?" he asked.

"I sure is, boss, I sure is," the Shark said in a deep-south movie accent as he rushed from the bar. He jumped into his car which was marked and scratched from its journeys through narrow, nearly impassible by-roads.

He urged the car forward at eighty miles an hour. The walls rushed past, the landscape was a moving thing. He passed car after car and finally he reached Oranmore. Now he slowed down. He cruised down the road by the sea at an easy pace. There was no sign of the caravan. Now he was coming to Galway proper. He followed the flow of traffic into Eyre Square. There in front of him was the caravan. He settled in behind it and followed. He felt uneasy in the city of Galway. The caravan rounded the square, passed the Great Southern Hotel and the Skeffington and turned down Shop Street past the Allied Irish bank which had once been Lynch's Castle. People waved to the Carneys as they passed down the street.

For Mrs Carney and the children, the sight of Galway was a glorious thing. They had journeyed across Ireland. They had had many adventures and now they were almost home. This was the mother's city. Her people had known it for twenty generations. They had carried on their business here in Irish. It was an Irish city and it was a European city and it was itself.

They could smell the sea.

Mrs Carney stopped the horse and caravan beside the medieval market close to St Nicholas's Church.

Her mind and her body were filled with delight. Against all the odds she had challenged fortune and won. Further west, not far from the market place, lay her home.

Envoi

hey looked at the richness about them. Everywhere there were stalls heaped with the wealth of the countryside. Vegetables lay in pyramids and circles on carts. There were large wheels of cheese, brown and creamy and strong, shaded by an awning. Beside this stall there was glazed and unglazed pottery, fired in some local kiln. Next, a variety of fish, cooled by lumps of ice, smelt of the sea. The market was a wonderful mixture of colour and sound and noise and scents. And then at the edge of the market Mrs Carney came upon her own people. She began to talk to them in Irish. They threw their arms about her and the women and men made her welcome. They asked her many questions.

"I am home now," she explained, "and my

children have come with me. We travelled all through Ireland to be here this Saturday for the market. There will be no returning to Dublin now. How is my father?"

"Well, but lonely. He has been waiting for many a day since your husband died," said one of her people.

"I could not come to him. It is a long story and a sad story."

"Well you'll have a long time to tell it and I'm sure it is full of wonder."

"It is full of wonder at the end, but not at the beginning."

"Then the ending is happy and that is important."

All might have ended there at the market place beside St Nicholas's Church. But suddenly there was a roar from the crowd as the Shark rushed at Mrs Carney. He had caught up with her at last. "That woman owes me. She has what is rightfully mine." And with that he grabbed her by the neck of her dress. It was his final mistake. The men caught him and would have brought their sticks heavily down upon his head but Mrs Carney restrained them.

"This man," she began in a calm, strong voice, "is the Shark. He has bled me of my substance and my money. He has pursued me through Ireland and never given either me or my children peace. He has given the children nightmares. I have paid him more than I ever owed him. He is the cause of my misery and the misery of many others."

By now an angry crowd had gathered around the Shark. He was caught like a rat in one of his own traps. The safety of Dublin and his tasteless house seemed a million miles away. The Galway men never took their eyes off him and their hands would from time to time tighten round their sticks. The Shark was beaten and he knew it. He suddenly felt very afraid. As he looked at the eyes of those about him he began to tremble. "There is nothing I want from this woman. The business between us is closed," he stuttered.

But the men were not satisfied. They wanted to take him aside and thrash him, but Mrs Carney broke in, "Leave him go. I will go to my people and let him go back to his own type."

And all the while the televison camera was recording what was happening.

The Shark, now a humiliated bully, turned and walked fearfully through the crowd. They formed a silent aisle for him to walk through. He got into his car and left Galway behind. He was beaten. He had let his anger lead him astray.

All that day the Carneys stayed in Galway. Everywhere they turned they met old friends of Mrs Carney who welcomed them. And that evening they climbed into the caravan for the final part of their journey. They clopped over the Corrib bridge where the muttering waters rush to the sea. They passed along by the wide and even sweep of Salthill and the immensity of Galway Bay. The sun was setting in its summer glory. There was peace everywhere. At the village of Barna the Carneys turned south to their own private sea.

The old man was smoking his pipe and looking at the ending of the day when he saw the caravan coming over the brow of the hill. He knew immediately that his daughter and her children had returned home. He waited for the caravan to enter the yard. There were tears in his eyes as he watched the children rush to him. He gathered them into his arms. And then he looked at his daughter. It was not necessary to speak. They understood what was in each other's heart.

They all looked at the great sea beyond the small private bay. It was tranquil and filled with the quiet light of evening. The coming and the going of the waves filled the air with its eternal sound. And out on the edge of the sky the evening star was hanging like a small lantern, a guide for ancient ships.

At last they turned from the great wonder of the sea and went indoors.